REBEL WIND

Brieanna Robertson

Whimsical Publications, LLC

Florida

Rebel Wind is a work of fiction. Names, characters, and incidents are the products of the author's imagination and are either fictitious or are used fictitiously. Any resemblance to actual events or persons, living or dead, is entirely coincidental.

To purchase the authorized electronic edition of *Rebel Wind*, visit
www.whimsicalpublications.com

Cover art by Traci Markou
Editing by Jessica Keiley

ISBN-13: 978-1-940707-84-6

Published by
Whimsical Publications, LLC
Florida

Jackson looked down, hurt mirrored in his eyes. "You just bailed on me, Hayden. You rode away and never looked back, and you haven't even cared enough to come visit me, like, ever."

"I'm here now."

"Yeah, because you ran out of excuses. I could hardly believe my eyes when you showed up in my driveway. Not when you didn't even come to my college graduation."

Hayden swallowed hard. "My work wouldn't let me off."

"Or when I graduated from the police academy."

"I did try to come to that!" he exclaimed. "My car broke down in Arizona!"

Jackson shook his head and heaved a defeated-sounding sigh. "Yeah, I know, you always had plenty of good excuses. Tons of things that were more important than me. What you never realized is that, while you thought taking care of me was sucking out all the life in your soul, I idolized you." Hayden opened his mouth to protest, but Jackson held up his hand. "Save it. Don't deny that's how you felt because I know you did. I'm not stupid. I can figure things out." He sighed again and some of the anger went out of him. "I know you did what you had to do, and I know you'd do it again, so don't give me the speech, okay? I also know it wasn't what you wanted. It was just the hand you got dealt, and you're a good person so you did what had to be done. You've always been kind and you've always been honorable, and I am forever grateful for the fact that you took the responsibility upon yourself to be my guardian. But…" He looked up at him and Hayden's heart splintered at the sorrow in his little brother's eyes. He gave a small, sad smile. "Do you know why I got that Metallica album on my arm? Because some of my most annoying memories are of when I would wake up to James Hetfield growling away instead of an alarm clock. And I'd stagger out into the kitchen to yell at you about it and there you'd be, in your badass bandanna and your black jeans with chains hanging out of the pocket, making me oatmeal and scrambled eggs. Those annoying memories also happen to me my happiest. Because you were all I had, and I knew you'd always be there. And then one day, you weren't."

Hayden exhaled a long, slow breath, wondering if he could disappear into the floorboards. He had never felt so low or small in his entire life. "Jack," he murmured. "I'm so sorry. I had no idea..." But he knew that was a lie. He'd always known. He'd just been too much of a chicken to face the guilt.

"You're the only family I have, Hayden," Jack said softly. "Mom and Dad were taken away from us involuntarily. *You* took you away from me. They can't come back. You can, but you don't."

There was nothing in the world that anyone could have said to him that would have hurt him worse than those words. And it was because he knew they were true. Brutal, but true.

"I don't begrudge you having your own life," Jack continued. "But does that mean you have to disassociate yourself with everything from the one you used to have? Even me?"

A long silence stretched between them, mainly because the pain constricting Hayden's chest made it impossible for him to speak. Finally, Jack grabbed the shirt back again.

"You should leave it off." Hayden forced the words passed his lips. "Shelby's eyes lit up when she saw all your work."

Jack arched an eyebrow. "You think?"

Hayden nodded. "Jack," he said as his brother pushed past him to get out of the cubicle. His voice sounded as strangled as it felt. "I-I'm sorry. I—"

This time, Jack's sigh sounded like resignation. "I know, Hayden. Let's not make a federal case out of it, okay? I don't want to ruin the day, or your trip for that matter. Let's just forget it." He threw the curtain aside and stepped out.

Just forget it? How could he? He'd crushed his little brother, the person he loved the most in the whole world, because of his own selfishness, because of his own fear. He'd made him feel abandoned and not good enough. It would have hurt less if someone had bashed his knees in with a sledge hammer. Because it was all true.

He'd never hated himself more than he did at that moment.

To Tawny—
My TST, my "Shelby," my longtime friend and almost-sister.
Here's to all our adventures and more to come—because we are "superly awesome."

Also by
Brieanna Robertson

Serendipity Series

The Road Less Traveled
Better Than Chocolate
Dark Masterpiece
Paladin
Stage Presents

Stand Alone Books

Amaranth of the Wild Things
The One Inside the Looking Glass
Confessions From A Studio Apartment

Chapter One

The leaves were just starting to change colors, dotting the thick pine trees with hints of yellow and orange as he descended the Sierras. Just past Truckee, CA, Hayden maneuvered his Harley down the winding mountain road with mixed feelings about returning to his hometown.

Jackson had been bugging him for years to come to Street Vibrations, the biker rally held in Reno, NV every September. Hayden usually avoided it, telling his brother that he could only afford to go to Sturgis. It was true, in part. He did prefer to go to Sturgis, but considering he'd been living only two hours away in Sacramento for the past year, and Jackson was offering to let him stay at his place for the weekend, Hayden really didn't have a viable excuse this time around.

He felt like a jerk for even trying to get out of it. Jackson had come to see him who knew how many times at all of the locations he'd wandered through over the past seven years. Arizona, New Mexico, Oregon, and most of California—Hayden wasn't a person who liked to stay in one place for too long. He started to get restless if he put down too many roots, started to feel like the life was being sucked out of him. Jackson had visited all of his stopping places, and Hayden hadn't been home once.

It wasn't his brother he didn't want to see. He always had a good time with Jack, even if he was a bit of a nut-job now and again. Reno just had way too many ghosts in it to suit him. Ghosts he didn't really want to face if he could help it.

But he only had one little brother, and he never asked much. He'd been putting him off for years, and there came a point when a person stopped sounding credible and just started sounding like a douchebag. Hayden didn't want Jackson to start thinking it was *him* he had a problem with, or like everything else was more important than the only member he had left of his family.

So, here he was, riding back into Reno, a place he had ridden out of without a backward glance seven years prior. The highway was littered with other random bikers—he'd been seeing them all the way through the mountains—all heading to the rally. He heaved a sigh and tried to will away some of the apprehension tightening his chest.

He tried to tell himself that this wasn't going to be a big deal. He was just going to party for the weekend with others of his kind, and have a nice visit with his brother. There was no need to worry about issues that had been buried a long time ago.

But he knew in the back of his mind, as much as he hated to admit it, that the past had a way of coming back from the dead, especially if it had never been properly buried in the first place. It was like a zombie, coming back to eat you alive. And deep down, he knew he couldn't run from it forever.

There had to be something she could throw, or someone she could strangle. If she could find some stray dynamite lying around somewhere, she'd be more than happy to blow her car to kingdom come.

"No, Shelby, I don't need you to come and get me," Gina said to her sister on the phone as she leaned up against the side of her defeated vehicle. "Yes, I'm sure. I'm fine. I'm just gonna sit here...and bake...in the hundred degree heat while I wait for friggin' Triple A to get their butts in gear and send me a tow truck." Not that that was going to happen anytime soon. She'd already been waiting out there for an hour and a half. "Yeah, I called Mom. She's coming to give me a ride home after my car gets towed to my mechanic... I don't know what's wrong with it. I think I blew my transmission. Look, I have to go. Just call me and let me know when you find out about your brakes so I can figure out if I still get to go on vacation."

She hung up and heaved an annoyed sigh. Of course she was wearing all black, on the hottest day of the year. And there was virtually no shade anywhere on the street she had managed to lope onto. Friggin' awesome.

It had been one of those weeks. Work had sucked and her neighbors had been keeping her up all hours of the night with their wild, drunken, druggie parties that sent pounding, thumping hip hop music pulsating through her apartment at three a.m. She'd come home two days that week with so much pot smoke seeping into her apartment she could have gotten a contact high. There had also been gunshots at one point. She'd called the cops one night, but that hadn't really done much good and they were still driving her nuts.

Not only that, but she and Shelby had been planning their annual road trip for the past three months, and were due to go in a week's time to Ft. Bragg, CA. They were going to spend a week lounging by the ocean, camping in the redwoods, and enjoying some much-needed relaxation.

That was until Shelby's car, the much more reliable of the two vehicles, had decided to freak out in every annoying way possible. After getting it road worthy, her brakes had promptly decided to go out, and now her roommate was trying to replace them, but was having difficulty doing it. At this point, they had no idea if they were actually going to make it out of town.

Gina's car was definitely a no-go. It had been having weird problems that no mechanic in Reno seemed to be able to figure out, and after putting more money into parts than she even wanted to think about, the poor thing had finally thrown in the towel on her way home from work today.

Right off the freeway exit, it had decided it no longer wanted to shift gears or go above 20 MPH. Gina did not have the money to fix a blown transmission. Not on her salary. She had always been a work-to-live type of person, not a live-to-work one. So her job as a personal assistant to various wealthy people paid the bills and let her do the things she loved, but didn't heap a lot of extra cash in her wallet.

She spotted her mom's red Jeep coming up the road and pushed away from her car to go meet her just as the tow truck finally came around the corner. Gina rolled her eyes and waited for the truck driver to get out. She gave him instructions on where to take her car, then climbed into her mom's Jeep.

Her mother instantly gave her a bottle of water and offered a granola bar. Gina took the water, but scrunched her nose at the thought of having to eat another granola bar. It was her mom's emergency food supply, always used in situations where one of her daughters might need to refuel. Gina had eaten so many granola bars over the course of her life, just looking at them made her want to heave. True, she hadn't eaten since nine that morning and it was now three, but she still wasn't hungry enough to suffer through an oat and nut monstrosity.

She spent the short ride to the garage griping while her mom listened patiently, and when Gina told her mechanic what had happened, his exclamation of, "Oh man, that's not good!" was somehow less than encouraging.

"So, you and Shelby leave next week, right?" Gina's mom asked as they left the car at the garage and headed back to Gina's apartment.

Gina sighed. "Let's hope so. We've made all the reservations and I could really use the vacation. But right now, things aren't looking so hot." She absently sniffed at her armpit and made a face. "I stink. Not surprising after standing out in the sun for a hundred years. All I want to do is go home and take a shower. And eat something." She was so hungry her stomach felt like it was going to start devouring her internal organs.

"You sure you don't want that granola bar?" her mom prodded.

Gina grimaced. No, definitely not the granola bar. She'd let her stomach have her spleen before she ate that thing. She could live without her spleen.

She heaved a sigh of relief as they pulled up to the duplex in front of Gina's tiny apartment. Her studio was in the back alley. It was dilapidated, cramped, and older than dirt, but it was cheap, and it was home. And right now, it seemed like the Promised Land.

"Thanks, Mom," she muttered as she climbed out of the car.

"No problem. Call me when you find out what's going on with your car. And tell your sister to do the same."

Gina nodded and made her way up the driveway that led to the courtyard as her mom pulled away. She had only taken maybe about five steps when she rounded the corner and a police officer popped out at her. She jumped back with a squeak of surprise.

"Sorry, ma'am, but you can't go back there." He was tall and fat, the typical donut-cop, and he was trying his hardest to be intimidating. That was difficult to do with his red hair and PC-gamer glasses.

Gina frowned and tried to peer over his bulky shoulder. "But I live here," she stated pitifully. All she wanted to do was disappear into her house. Was that really so much to ask? She was sweating, stinky, and starving. And her patience level had bottomed out a long time ago.

The cop eyeballed her for a second like she was somehow involved with whatever was happening. "Which apartment do you live in?"

"Number five." She could see it right past him. Her door was beckoning. So close, and yet so far.

The cop stink-eyed her again, then picked up his walkie-talkie and started muttering into it right as Gina's phone started to blare. She jumped, her nerves shot beyond all belief, and she fumbled through her purse to answer it.

"Hello?" she practically shouted, taking a couple steps away from the police officer.

"Gina? What is going on? There are cops everywhere back here!"

She frowned at her mother's surprised voice and she shot a glance back at the cop keeping her from retreating into seclusion. "Yeah, well, they won't let me get into my apartment at the moment either. Can you see what's going on?"

"No, but the street is all blocked off and there are cops all over back here by your neighbors'. There's a paddy wagon and everything!"

Gina rolled her eyes. Well, wonderful. "Maybe they did a drug bust." Finally. That was great, but the fact that it was keeping her from getting into her apartment was really annoying.

"They won't let you in? Do you need me to come and get you?"

"Ma'am?"

Gina turned back around to face the cop. "No, Mom, it's fine. I've gotta go. I'll call you back in a little bit." She hung up and returned to where the police officer was standing with his hands on his hips.

"All right, go ahead and go in," he said, giving her a look like he was doing her a huge favor.

She raised an eyebrow. "Thanks. Is everything all right?"

He nodded gravely in a way that let her know she wouldn't be getting any more information out of him. She fought rolling her eyes again and pushed past him to cross the courtyard. She couldn't unlock her door fast enough.

Once inside, she all but slammed it shut, locked it, and leaned back against it with a huge sigh of relief. Finally, she was home. Carless, frustrated, with lord only knew what going on next door—and probably nursing sunstroke—but home. And she didn't have anywhere else she needed to be for the rest of the night.

A shower was in order. And right after that, it was time for dinner, a glass—or a gallon—of wine, and her favorite pair of monkey shorts.

She pushed away from the door, pulled off her black baseball hat, flung it aside, and headed toward the bathroom. Oh yes, it was definitely a wine and monkey shorts kind of evening.

Chapter Two

Despite his reservations about coming back to Reno, Hayden was filled with a sense of pride as he pulled into the driveway of his brother's newly purchased South Reno home. Jackson had done well for himself, which made Hayden feel like maybe he'd done something right. It was a good feeling, considering he'd raised Jack from age twelve—not the easiest age bracket to cope with. Especially when he had been seventeen himself. It hadn't been easy, and Jack hadn't always been a cooperative teen. It had been difficult riding the fine line between big brother and parent substitute, and Hayden had felt like he'd botched most of it most of the time.

But despite the troubles of teenage angst, Jack had graduated, gone to the University of Nevada Reno, then on to the police force. This last year, he had bought a brand new home in one of the nicer parts of town, and Hayden felt strangely out of place as he looked at his rebel Harley parked next to his brother's squad car. Even Jack's yard looked pristine. All it needed was a white picket fence and a dog.

Jackson's slice of the American Dream contrasted so greatly with Hayden's gypsy lifestyle that it made him feel weird, like the black sheep that should go graze in someone else's pasture. He couldn't quite name the odd, achy feeling that settled in around his heart.

Luckily, he didn't have to think about it for long because Jack came running out the door, snapping Hayden out of his reverie.

"Dude, you really came!" he shouted. He didn't even give Hayden a chance to take his helmet off before he caught him in a bear hug that almost crushed his ribs.

Hayden's breath wheezed out of him like an accordion and he returned his brother's hug, slapping him on the back in what he hoped seemed like enthusiasm. In all reality, it was a silent plea to let him go so he could take in some oxygen.

"Are you really that shocked?" he choked out after Jackson finally released him and he was able to remove his helmet.

Jackson snorted. "Uh, yeah. I seriously thought you'd come up with about ten million last minute excuses."

Well, geez. Way to make him feel like a turd. He glanced over his clean-cut brother, and ran his hand over his own scruffy jaw. They even looked like polar opposites, right down to his brother's preppy button-down shirt and tan slacks and Hayden's kick-you-to-the-moon, steel-toed boots and leather jacket. How come he'd never noticed that before? And how come it suddenly made him feel so awkward?

Jackson clapped and rubbed his hands together. "All right! Let's get this started! I'll give you the grand tour." He swept his arm to indicate his home. "Get you settled in, then go grab some dinner downtown maybe. I have to work for a bit after that. They called me in to do a patrol for one of the other guys who is puking his guts out or something. But that's not that big a deal. You can just come with me."

"Is that allowed?"

Jackson frowned as he started back toward his front door. "Who's gonna know? It's just a patrol. Oh!" He stopped abruptly and grinned like a devil. "I *have* to show you this. You're gonna crap your pants."

Hayden arched an eyebrow.

Jackson ran inside for a second and must have activated the garage door because it started to rise. He ran back out again and put his hands on his hips in a proud display as the door slowly revealed an obnoxiously red sports bike. Hayden tried to suppress his grimace, but failed.

"Isn't it awesome?" Jack cried. "Now I can ride with you!"

Hayden knew his expression was pained. He could feel it. "Jack, why did you buy this thing?"

"Um, so I could ride with you, like I just said."

"But..." He heaved a sigh and ran his hand through his hair. "Jack, this is not a motorcycle."

Jackson frowned and looked at it as if it had suddenly morphed shape. "Uh…yeah it is."

Hayden almost whimpered. "Dude, the only way I would let you get away with this is if you were a Ninja assassin."

Jackson's deadpan expression spoke volumes. "I *am* a Ninja assassin," he muttered.

"Oh yeah?"

"Yeah." He practically spat the word out. "And just so you know, I would rather have a bike that gets me somewhere instead of only making a lot of noise." He started to head back inside.

"I wouldn't even qualify that as a bike—"

"Shut it!" he shouted, and Hayden smirked as Jack's disgruntled front slipped away to reveal his unbridled enthusiasm. "Come on, bro! We're wasting time! Virginia City with Troy tomorrow, right?" He shouted this excitedly over his shoulder while jaunting back into his house.

Hayden smirked. Jack's elation was contagious, he had to admit, and how could he rain on his parade when he was obviously so happy to see him? He felt like a jerk for putting off visiting all these years.

With a sigh, Hayden grabbed his things off the back of his bike and headed in after his brother. He tried not to think about the pending trip up to Virginia City with his old best friend either. That had all been Jack's doing. He'd looked the guy up and invited him along, knowing that he rode a bike also. He'd thought it would make Hayden feel more comfortable and have a better time, but in all reality, it just made him feel more out of his element.

Troy, a year older than Hayden, had left Reno after high school to go to school back east. They'd kept in tentative contact over the years, exchanging the required hey-how-are-yous that happened when too much time passed. They spoke on the phone maybe once a year, and sent an email now and then. Troy had apparently moved back to Reno three years ago, but it was going to be weird hanging out with him after all this time. What were they supposed to talk about? Troy owned a bar now. He'd found his place, set up his life. Hayden was still wandering, searching for his path.

Up until this point, he'd always thought wandering *was* his path, but being back here again, knowing the people in his life had become so settled and established, made him feel like maybe he'd only been fooling himself. What was it he kept searching for? He didn't even know.

Being back here made him feel itchy, like he was uncomfortable in his own skin and needed to get away, back out on the open road, back to freedom. He'd never wanted the life his brother had chosen. He'd never wanted the house and the fence and the dog and kids. So then, why did being here make him feel like he was somehow missing out on something? It was confusing at best.

With a sigh, he set his stuff down in Jack's spare bedroom and tried to banish his weird reflective thoughts. He was here to see his brother and ride around town with a bunch of other bikers. He could give himself therapy later.

"So, this is what you do all day, huh?" Hayden teased, running his hand along the dash of Jack's squad car. "Drive around and, what, look for criminals or something?" He tossed him a playful grin.

Jackson rolled his eyes and gave him a bland expression. "No, I don't *only* do patrols. And I'm only doing this right now to fill in for Billy. I took the days off that you were going to be here. I shouldn't have to be working at all."

Hayden smiled to himself, feeling warm knowing that his brother had gone to the trouble to get work off just because he was coming into town. "Okay, fine, so what do you do usually?"

Jackson sighed. "Right now I mostly do traffic stuff, unfortunately. Have to work your way up and all." He shot him a glance. "But that doesn't make me any less of a cop."

Hayden smirked and reached over to slug his brother in the shoulder.

Jack let out a pitiful-sounding moan and his arm drooped while he steered his car with the other hand. "Dude, Hayden, you gave me a friggin' dead arm. That's my gun arm too. Nice."

Hayden laughed. "Just wanted to see how well they trained you in self-defense at the Academy."

He snorted. "Well, they taught me how to disarm and incapacitate someone. Taught me how to shoot someone in the head, but I must have missed the day they taught how to fend off obnoxious older brothers." He balanced the wheel on his knees and reached over to rub his shoulder.

"Oh yeah, that's real safe," Hayden grumbled.

Jackson glowered at him while his radio started to make some incoherent noise. He put his hands back on the wheel and grabbed the receiver end. He rattled off some police jargon, then glanced over at Hayden. "Hey, hold tight for a bit. There's a couple officers requesting backup and I'm the closest, so I'm gonna respond."

Hayden frowned. "Aren't they gonna get pissed that I'm in the car?"

Jackson shrugged. "You're fine. Don't worry about it." He flashed him a devious grin. "Now, check this out. This is why I wanted the job." He turned his lights and siren on and parted traffic like Moses at the Red Sea.

Hayden chuckled and sat back in his seat to enjoy the ride.

"No, it's actually not my transmission," Gina said to her mom on the phone while she putzed around in the bathroom, tidying up and what-not. "I dunno. Some sensor thing. I don't care. I'm just happy it isn't going to cost me a couple grand... Yeah, her brakes are fine. Her roommate ended up getting them fixed, so as far as right now is concerned, vacation is still a go... She's at work, Mom. She'll call you when she gets off. You know she will. She always does."

Gina frowned when she suddenly heard loud pounding on the door of the apartment next to her.

"Geez," she muttered into the phone, "there is still action going on next door. Do you know that earlier today I saw three degenerates skulking around here? Probably looking for their stash. I don't know what happened, but they suddenly took off like their lives depended on it."

"Police! Open the door! We have a search warrant!"

Gina's eyes bulged. "Oh my gosh!" she breathed. She instinctively dropped down to a crouch. "The cops are raiding the apartment next door!" She crawled over and shut off her bathroom light. She had no idea why. It was easier to spy in the dark. Slowly, she duck-waddled back over to the window to try and hear what was going on. Her mother was asking questions. "Shh!" she demanded in a whisper. "I can't hear. Hold on a second!" She heard muttered voices outside and saw the beam of a flashlight reflecting in the darkness of the alley. "I don't know what's going on. I can't tell... Look, lemme call you back." She barely gave her mom a chance to answer before she ended the call and continued to strain her ears in an attempt to hear what was taking place.

She heard at least three different voices, and then it sounded as if two of them came up closer to her window.

"What's the layout in there?"

"I don't know. I heard voices, though. And the light went off."

Gina winced. Crap. Bad move. Now they thought she was hiding a fugitive or something.

"No, I can't see anything... Dude, do me a favor and go see if anyone lives on the other side."

"Jack, what the—"

"Can you just do it, please?"

Gina all but commando crawled out of the bathroom, pulled herself back into a standing position, headed through her bedroom and out toward the living room. She didn't know what was going on, but she was pretty sure hanging out in the bathroom and eavesdropping wasn't going to be beneficial.

As she rounded the corner into her living room and kitchen, her gaze traveled to the screen door, which was open due to the unseasonably sweltering temperature of the day. As if by magic, a man manifested from the darkness and came up onto her porch.

Gina screamed, her heart leaping into her throat, and she grabbed the closest thing she could use as a weapon, which happened to be an authentic medieval spear propped up in her hallway.

The stranger instantly held his hands out in front of him. "I'm sorry, I'm sorry!"

"You scared the crap out of me!" she spat, still clutching the spear in one hand as she ventured closer to the door.

"I apologize. Really. The—" He pointed vaguely toward

the alley. "The police, they…" He drew in a deep breath and seemed to collect himself. "I need to check out the layout of your apartment, ma'am."

She arched an eyebrow and stood straight, resting the spear point-up on the ground and leaning her weight against it. She could see enough of him through the screen door to suddenly wish she was wearing just about anything but her faded, beat-up, too-short, monkey boxers.

He was dressed in jeans and a black T-shirt and had dark blond, rebelliously wavy hair that fell to his broad shoulders. His jaw was square and sporting about two days' worth of bad-boy stubble. "You're a cop?" she asked in disbelief.

"*I'm* not, no. I'm just…" He scratched at the back of his head. "Helping." He gave a feeble shrug. "Can I please come in? I'm sorry I frightened you."

She eyeballed him for a few seconds and stepped closer to the door. "Lemme see your badge."

"I told you, I'm not a cop. The dudes in the alley are. I'm pretty sure I'm not even supposed to be here. I feel like I'm with those cops from *Superbad*. I'm on friggin' vacation!"

She laughed in spite of herself at his frustration. She gave him another once-over before she tentatively unlocked her screen, but she leveled her spear at him. She didn't have any creepy vibes, but one could never be too careful. "What were you doing sneaking up here underneath my search light anyway? It was like you materialized out of nowhere." She stepped back to a safe distance as he entered.

"Again, I apologize." He stopped for a second and stared at her weapon. "Are you really going stab me with a…spear?"

Now that he was inside and in the light, she could see that his eyes were mouth-wateringly blue, and his hair glinted golden in places like it had been sun-kissed. He had a tattoo peeking out from underneath his shirtsleeve. He was absolutely delicious in the most reckless way. She shrugged. "A girl has to protect herself somehow."

He glanced at her spear again, gave her a strange expression, and then started out of the room. He stopped short when he saw her wall full of swords, daggers, and other ancient weaponry. "Well, geez, I guess you had your pick."

She smirked. "I collect medieval weapons."

He threw her a disarming smile over his shoulder as he

disappeared around the corner and she stifled a groan. She ran her fingers through her hair several times, knowing it was useless. She hadn't bothered to do anything with it after she'd gotten out of the shower. It was probably lying on top of her head like a dark brown, dead animal. And she was on her third glass of wine. She probably smelled like an alcoholic, and her lips and teeth were probably tinged with purple. This was a nightmare.

He came back into the room suddenly and smiled again. His teeth were gorgeous, and he had just enough of a dimple in his left cheek to make her want to drool. "Thanks. Sorry about all of that." He passed by her and pointed at her weapon. "You can put that away now."

She blinked in surprise. Up until now, she had forgotten she still held it. What was she doing standing in her kitchen propped on a spear like an aborigine on walkabout? Yeah, she just kept racking up the points. She felt heat rush into her cheeks and she gave him a meager smile, but kept holding onto it like a lifeline. She shrugged. "How do I know you're safe? You're not a cop and you just wandered on into my house. The spear stays."

Faint surprise registered on his features, but it was chased away by a small smile. As he turned to go, his gaze rested for a moment on the shelf full of dragon and fairy statues and art, which were located right next to an oil painting of Tuscany and a shelf of pictures of everywhere she had ever traveled. For some reason, this brought a grin to his lips that lit up the entire room. "You're kind of all across the board, aren't you?" He glanced back at her with the most roguish twinkle in his eyes.

She shrugged as she felt her face burn hotter. "I like to travel. I like history... I really just like to experience as much as I can out of life."

At her words, the roguish twinkle turned into something more smoldering. He didn't say anything, but he stared at her long enough to make her exceedingly uncomfortable. When she glanced away, he flashed a smile and gave a short nod. "All right, have a good night, miss. Sorry again about all the fuss."

He let himself out and Gina stood there for a moment, feeling ridiculous. She heaved a sigh and then glanced down at her chest. Oh great. Yeah, she'd totally spaced the fact that she'd been wearing a white tank top...with no bra. And, of course, her nipples were totally pointing to the way out. *What—the—hell?* She whimpered. This day just kept getting better and better.

She snatched her phone off the arm of the sofa and stabbed her mother's number in. "Oh my gosh!" she all but shouted when her mom picked up. "The hottest guy just came to my door and I'm braless with no makeup on whatsoever. My hair is a disaster, my lips are probably purple, and I'm in my monkey shorts! My *monkey shorts*, Mom!" Her mother's laughter did not help matters. "Oh yeah, and I almost speared him like a shish kabob!"

She put her spear down and headed back toward her bathroom, wanting to look in the mirror, knowing she was going to be horrified. She flung the door open only to find a flashlight beam directed straight through her bathroom window. She screamed again. "Are you for real?" she screeched.

"What? What is it?" her mom queried.

Gina heaved a sigh. "Mom, I'll call you back." She hung up on her poor confused mother...again.

"Hey, I just heard something," one of the male voices said from outside her window.

Yeah, it was me, you idiot! She wished she could actually say that. This was getting ridiculous.

"Do you think someone is in there?"

"Yeah, someone is in there. It's that poor woman I just scared the daylights out of."

"No, I think this is the other apartment."

"I found firearms inside," came the third voice. "How do you get to that room?"

"It's the other apartment!"

"Go check again."

"What? Jack, go yourself! This is your job!"

Gina couldn't figure out who was who, but she wanted to hide in her shower at the thought of that gorgeous man coming back into her apartment. Maybe she should put a bra on. Or pull her hair up into a ponytail. Or brush her teeth... She sighed. It was no use. There was no time, and how obvious would that be anyway? He'd already seen her looking horrid. No sense in trying to hide it now.

Escaping from her bathroom again, and starting to feel like she was part of some three-ring circus, she entered her kitchen right as Mr. Hottie McHottie and another dude stepped back up onto her porch.

"Hi," Mr. McHottie said as he peered through her screen door. "Um...I'm really sorry, but we need to take one more look, all right? It's cool. He *is* a cop. Has a badge and everything. Please don't throw an axe at us or something."

She rolled her eyes.

"Do you know the man who lives next door, ma'am?" the other guy asked as they entered. He was most definitely a cop—blue uniform, gun belt, the whole nine yards.

Gina shook her head. "I just know he caused a lot of problems."

"And your bathroom is right next to..."

"Their bathroom. We share a wall. You keep shining your light into *my* bathroom."

He frowned and muttered something under his breath. "Mind if I take a look?"

"Be my guest," she grumbled. What did he expect to find in there? Refugees? Border jumpers? A meth lab? Good lord...

He started down the narrow hallway and had to turn sideways to avoid knocking all of her weapons off the wall. Gina stifled a giggle, and when she turned back around, her heart tripped over itself to see that Mr. McHottie's lovely baby blues were regarding her warmly. She chewed on her lip, feeling awkward, and the air around them seemed to thicken with tension.

Say something, Gina! she shouted at herself. *Don't stand here like an idiot! Open your mouth and say something witty!* When she looked down, all she could see were the monkeys on her shorts, staring up at her with enormous eyes, making faces, sticking their tongues out, mocking her...

She forced herself to meet his gaze again, and when she did, he grinned. "I'm Hayden, by the way," he stated. "And, uh, Barney Fife over there is my brother Jackson." He indicated the cop in her bathroom.

Some of the awkwardness dissipated, and she smiled. "I'm Gina." *Congratulations, stupid, you do have a voice.*

In the distance, the rumble of motorcycle engines could

be heard. She lived close to two main streets and the free-way. She'd be hearing that kind of thunder for the entire weekend.

He seemed to pick up on what she was listening to and his grin widened to the point that his dimple showed. "Do you like motorcycles at all?"

She tucked a few errant strands of hair behind her ears and nodded, then folded her arms self-consciously across her chest. "Yeah, my dad and sister are really into them. I rode once with my dad, but he didn't tell me to wear long pants, or not to get off on the muffler side."

Hayden sucked in his breath and winced, obviously know-ing where the story was headed.

"Yeah. Burned the crap out of my leg. It got all infected too. Was all gnarly and smelly and gangrenous." She stopped and averted her eyes. Yeah, that was sexy. Such a turn on, talking about necrotic flesh. Couldn't she just go to bed? Like, now? She cleared her throat and stole a glance back up at him again.

He was smirking. He stuffed his hands in his back pockets and rocked lightly on the balls of his feet. "Well, at least they didn't have to amputate."

She giggled. "Yeah, I didn't even go to a doctor. It's amazing what peroxide will do." She shrugged one shoulder in the most ridiculous, teenage-girl gesture she had done since she'd actually been a teenager. "Didn't really even leave much of a scar." Was this really the conversation they were having? The hottest man she'd basically ever seen was chilling out in her living room and she was talking about fes-tering burns?

"Well, uh…" He rubbed his hand along the back of his neck and looked down in the masculine version of teenager posturing. "I ride. A motorcycle." He cleared his throat in the same nervous way she had done, and she smiled as some of her unease slipped away. "That's actually why I'm here. I'm up for Street Vibrations. Tomorrow, me, a friend of mine, our Harleys, and Jack and his crotch-rocket—"

Gina burst out laughing at the slang term for a sports bike, having heard Shelby use it before. Her laughter caused Hayden to smile and heave a sigh that almost sounded like relief.

"We're riding up to Virginia City tomorrow for a bit. Are you planning on doing anything for Street Vibes?"

Gina snorted. "Are you kidding me? I don't have a choice. My sister Shelby considers it a national holiday."

He chuckled and adopted a much more relaxed stance, sidling just a little bit closer to her. Close enough that she got a whiff of his cologne. She didn't know what it was aside from wonderful. It was earthy and musky, masculine while still smelling divine.

"Would you...maybe...be interested in riding up with us? You and your sister?"

Gina arched an eyebrow playfully. "Are you really asking me out right now? After you raided my house, scared me to death, and I almost speared you?"

"Maybe," he said with an irresistible, boyish smile.

Gina's heart tumbled over itself a couple times and she bit her bottom lip shyly. This was officially the weirdest way she had ever been hit on. But like she was gonna say no. He was gorgeous. "Yeah, okay."

His grin was like daylight. "Really?"

She giggled. "Yeah. What time are you going? I'll have Shelby meet me over here."

"I think we're heading out around eleven. We can come and get you then. Your sister can ride with Jack or Troy, whoever she wants."

"This Troy guy has a Harley?"

He nodded.

"Yeah, she'll go with him. I don't think she'd be caught dead on a sports bike." She gave him what she hoped was a beguiling smile. "Does that mean I have to ride with your brother?"

He snorted. "Um, no. You'll ride with me. Of course."

She laughed softly. "Of course. What was I thinking?"

Jackson came back into the room then, shooting his brother a perplexed expression. "I think it's all figured out now," he said to Gina. "I'm really sorry about the inconvenience."

She shrugged and glanced back up at Hayden with a smile. "It's no inconvenience." There was a sparkle in his eye that she liked.

"All right, well, I'm pretty sure we won't be bothering you

again tonight, ma'am. Thank you for your cooperation." He grabbed Hayden's arm and started to haul him out after him.

"See you tomorrow," Hayden called over his shoulder with a wink.

Gina waved. Outside, as the two men rounded the corner, she could hear Jackson say, "Dude, did you seriously just pick up a chick?"

"Yeah, and?" came Hayden's response.

"Were...her lips...like purple?"

"Her lips were fine. I don't care what color they were. Go do your job."

She laughed and couldn't help the feeling of giddy elation that passed through her. Her day had sucked so famously and, somehow, had turned out not so terrible after all.

She grabbed her phone and started to dial her poor mom back as she made her way into her bathroom for the third time. While the phone rang, she glanced at her reflection in the mirror and heaved a sigh. Her dark brown hair was a tangled mess and she looked tired. And, yes, her lips and teeth really were tinged with purple.

Chapter Three

"So, is this Troy dude hot?" Shelby asked as she doused herself in about a gallon of perfume.

"How should I know? I never saw him. And crap." She snapped her fingers in an exaggerated fashion. "I totally forgot to get his criminal record while I was being picked up in my living room by a random stranger."

Shelby shot Gina a scowl and Gina giggled. It was a long-standing joke between her and her sister that Shelby only went after guys who were alcoholics or felons.

Shelby bent over and dangled her long, dark blonde hair upside-down while she cemented its curls in place with about a pound of hairspray. Gina frowned. "Did you seriously have a can of hairspray in your purse?"

Shelby righted herself and gave Gina an expression that said, *Well, duh.* "Gina, how long have you known me now? Oh right, since birth?" She stuffed her hairspray back into the black hole she called a designer bag. She fluffed her hair a bit and made sure her clothing was in place. For all the motorcycle-riding, football-loving, jeans and T-shirt wearing, beer drinking ways of her sister, Shelby was the girliest tomboy Gina had ever known. She was the only person who could belch the alphabet and light a fart on fire one second, then take a twenty-minute shower, slather every inch of her body with some froofy-smelling lotion, and go get a manicure in her favorite pair of Christian Louboutins. She was an enigma Gina doubted she would ever figure out, but she loved her.

"I can't believe you picked a biker up in your living room while his brother raided your neighbor," Shelby said.

Gina snorted. "After the day I had, I'm actually not that

surprised. So, everything is still a go for Fort Bragg?"

Shelby nodded. "Adam said my brakes are good to go now and the car is back in shape for a road trip."

"Awesome. At least one of us has a functioning vehicle. I was afraid our vacation was gonna bite it."

"Wouldn't that just be our luck? Seriously, why does fire and brimstone rain down every single time we try to take a vacation?"

It was true. They had survived flat tires, transmission problems, cats with worms, flesh-eating mosquitoes, criminals on the loose, panic attacks, pissy friends, irate lesbians, bleeding feet, bad directions, less than hospitable weather, and drama untold. Aside from a zombie apocalypse, they had practically seen it all.

Gina shrugged. "Beats me. Makes for good stories, though."

A knock sounded on Gina's door and they both jumped, then tried to fly out the bedroom door at the same time. They bumped into each other and Gina scowled. "Dude, get out of the way," she said, giving her sister a shove.

"Potentially cute boy!" Shelby shouted.

Gina rolled her eyes, escaped past her overbearing sister, and got to the door only seconds before Shelby caught up. Before she opened it, she paused and turned back to her sister.

Shelby raised an eyebrow. "What?"

Gina looked down at the ensemble she had chosen to wear. She looked a bit more rock star than biker in a black tank that had a guitar with wings on it, jeans, and black leather wristbands on her right arm. Her dark hair was pulled back into a braid—practical for motorcycle riding. "Do I look okay?"

"You look fine."

Gina glanced over what Shelby was wearing and made an annoyed noise in her throat.

"What?"

"What? Gimme a break, Shelby. Look at you." She was in a pair of hip-hugger jeans that were practically glued to her butt and had her boobs stuffed into a leather biker vest—and *only* a leather biker vest—showing off her half-sleeve tattoo full of colorful butterflies.

"What?" Shelby repeated, looking over herself.

"Well, I guess I shouldn't care what I'm wearing. As soon as I open the door, everybody's gonna be staring at you. Your Jupiter-sized ta-tas are practically oozing out of that thing. How'd you even get them in there?"

Shelby gasped and put her hands over her breasts. "Don't be mean!"

Gina raised an eyebrow and shrugged. "I'm not being mean. I'm stating a fact. If one of those puppies breaks free, someone's gonna lose an eye."

"Now you really are being mean! At least I have boobs and not two bug bites masquerading as boobs."

Now it was Gina's turn to gasp. She covered her breasts the same way Shelby had done in an affronted gesture. She narrowed her eyes. "That was below the belt. More than a handful is a waste."

"Well then you'd better hope the dude has small hands. And you know what they say about small hands."

"That's fine 'cause you only like guys with small brains."

Shelby huffed and folded her arms. "Really? Come on, Gina! You're always getting hit on, and guys have moved from out of state to come date you! This is my favorite time of year when I feel like I can really be myself, and you're gonna rag on me for it?"

Gina held her arms out to the sides. "All I'm saying is that I may as well just go put on a burlap sack. My date isn't gonna even notice me once you come into his line of sight. I don't know why I bothered at all, and seriously, how practical is that outfit? If you wreck, your tattoo is going to be scraped off by the asphalt."

Shelby gasped again, louder than before, and she hit Gina in the arm. "Why would you even say something like that? Take it back! Erase, erase, erase!"

Gina fought a smirk at her sister's usage of one of their childhood games.

"Why are you freaking out? You look *fine*," Shelby continued. "Besides, you already tried to spear the guy and he asked you out anyway. Just open the door."

"But—"

"Open the door!"

Gina made a growling noise in her throat and spun to obey. Three bewildered-looking men stood on the other side.

One was Hayden, looking all too mouth-watering in his leather jacket and jeans. He had on a necklace that looked Native American in design and it lent him an even more roguish, bad-boy appearance. Gina's heart did some kind of twitterpated dance.

She opened the screen door and smiled at them. "Hey, guys, this is my sister Shelby."

Hayden shook Shelby's hand. "I'm Hayden, this is Troy." He pointed to the guy on his left—tall, muscular arms, with a buzz cut and a shaggy kind of heavy metal goatee. He looked tough as nails. Right up Shelby's alley. "And this is my brother Jackson."

Shelby's ears perked at that. "Jackson? Like on *Sons of Anarchy*? Do people call you Jax?"

Jackson wasn't paying much attention to any of the conversation. His eyes were too glued to Shelby's cleavage.

Hayden frowned. "Jackson." He snapped his fingers in front of his all but drooling brother's face. "Jack!"

Jackson shook himself and looked up at Shelby with something close to worship in his eyes. "Hi, I'm Jackson." He grasped blindly for her hand.

"Right, we covered this," she said, but took his hand and shook it anyway.

"We usually call him Jack," Hayden supplied. "I don't think he's ever watched *Sons of Anarchy*."

Gina shrugged. "That's okay, neither have I." It was Shelby's favorite TV show, all about a biker gang. The lead character was her "future-baby-daddy," as she referred to him.

"Are you going to ride with me?" Jackson asked.

"Jack, the girl wants to ride on a *motorcycle,* not on your toy bike," Hayden nettled.

Jackson bristled. "How about I give you a ride down to the station?" He shot his brother a scathing glower. "I'm sure I could come up with some fake charge for them to hold you on."

Hayden raised an eyebrow and folded his arms. "Yeah? Try it and I'll tell your captain about your *Keystone Cops* routine last night."

Jackson's average-handsome face flushed with color and he averted his gaze to the ground while Shelby sidled over to Troy. Hayden chuckled and bent toward Gina's ear as she exited her apartment and locked the door. "You look wonderful," he practically purred. "And for the record, those are definitely not bug bites, and more than a handful *is* a waste."

Gina's eyes widened and she looked up into his playful blue eyes. "You guys heard all of that?"

He chuckled, causing his dimple to deepen. "Every word."

She groaned and heat flooded her face. "I should just ride with Jackson. We're probably the exact same shade of red."

"Close," he said with soft, sexy laughter. "And his bike is red, too. Fitting. So...looks like your sister likes my friend."

Gina watched as Shelby engaged in an advanced level of flirting with Troy while Jackson kept inserting himself into the conversation and trying to inch closer to her. The poor guy looked rather out of place in his long-sleeved, button-down shirt and blue jeans. Even the hole in the knee looked strategically placed. Why in the world was he wearing long sleeves in the first place? It was supposed to be somewhere around eighty degrees. And it was black, no less. She could understand Hayden and Troy's leather gear. That was a statement. But Jackson's wardrobe choice was lost on her. "Yeah...well, Troy is definitely her type," she finally said. "Is he single?"

"I think so."

"Criminal record?"

"I think he had a misdemeanor for failing to show up to a court date regarding a parking ticket."

Gina shrugged. "I imagine that'll be good enough for her." At Hayden's raised eyebrow, she giggled. "Long story. We ready to go?"

He nodded and clapped his hands. "Come on, girls, we're burning daylight!" His brother shot him a scowl, Shelby jumped up and down while declaring how excited she was, and Troy shifted his weight in a lazy, nonchalant movement, but he didn't actually say anything.

Gina looked up at Hayden, who was smiling down at her. "You ready?" he asked.

She loved the roguish twinkle in his eyes. "Ready as I'll ever be."

"Do you trust me?" His dimple deepened as he teased her.

She arched an eyebrow. "Strangely...yes."

"Excellent." He held his hand out to her. "Let's ride."

Chapter Four

Gina knew she'd enjoy riding on the back of a motorcycle. She had loved the freedom of the wind against her face and the feel of the sun on her skin when she'd ridden with her dad, but she hadn't really anticipated how much different the experience would be riding behind Hayden. It was one thing to clutch onto her father while they zoomed around the Reno streets, but another thing entirely to wrap her arms around the waist of a completely hot man while twisting and turning up a rural, two-lane highway that slithered up a mountain. Especially when said man kept leaning back into her at every available moment.

She resisted the urge to rest her head on his shoulder for two reasons. Number one, she would miss the wild desert scenery going by. Number two, regardless of how attracted she was to Hayden—or how good he smelled—she wasn't going to fawn all over him like she'd never seen a man before. So what if her heart was pounding at the virile, masculine nearness of him for the *entire* ride? He didn't need to know that.

They arrived at Virginia City an hour or so later. The Old West-styled streets were lined with bikes, and men and women in leather and chaps could be seen in every direction. Gina climbed off Hayden's bike and removed her helmet, attempting to smooth her hair so it didn't look horrendous.

"We're all gonna have helmet head," Hayden said as he tossed out his own golden waves. "Don't stress about it." He flashed her a playful grin, then turned to Troy and Shelby, who were also dismounting. Jack came zipping in a few moments later.

"Finally, you get here," Hayden nettled. "I thought you were supposed to be on the fast bike."

Jackson pulled his helmet off and wiped the sweat from his forehead with the back of his sleeve. "Dude, did you even see those hairpin turns? I thought I was gonna go straight off the mountain and into a ravine."

Shelby raised an eyebrow. Her hair was still immaculate despite the helmet—courtesy of the twenty tons of Aqua Net. "Has he been riding long?" she asked, aiming her question toward Hayden.

"No, I haven't," Jackson spat. He wiped his face again. "And what is it, like five hundred degrees? Oh my gosh, I'm baking."

Hayden snorted. "You're the Einstein who decided to wear a long-sleeved, *black* shirt. What is the matter with you?"

Jackson scowled, but remained silent.

"All right, I'm hungry," Gina declared. "I barely had a breakfast."

"I know a place that's decent," Troy finally said.

"Lead the way!" Shelby exclaimed. She fell into step with Troy, trying to engage him in more conversation, and Jackson trailed behind, trying to throw in his two cents, much like he had been doing back at the house.

Hayden sighed and ran a hand through his hair. "This should be interesting," he said, glancing down at Gina. She laughed softly as they started after the others. "You know, I don't really remember Troy being so silent."

"When was the last time you saw him?" Gina asked.

"High school," he replied with a chuckle.

"Oh, well that might explain it. Time changes everyone." He frowned thoughtfully at her words and grew quiet. She wondered about that reaction, but didn't press the issue.

They ate at a hole-in-the-wall restaurant where Hayden and Troy caught up a bit and Shelby tried in vain to catch Troy's interest while Jackson tried in vain to catch Shelby's. Gina had never seen anything quite like it and it started to give her a headache. She couldn't figure out why her sister seemed so taken with Troy. He was shaping up to have the personality of a potato, and he spent most of lunch on his cell phone in some form or another. He claimed it was business-related, but Gina still thought it was kind of tacky.

And Jackson's puppy eyes were almost as nauseating as the way Shelby kept overcompensating for the fact that Troy was ignoring her by being as loud as possible. Although, Troy's eyes didn't seem to be able to look at any other part of Shelby's anatomy aside from her boobs, so maybe her shouting at him was necessary.

All Gina knew was that when Shelby suggested they all take a train ride after lunch, she was all for it. Shelby could deal with her man-sandwich and Gina and Hayden could have some one-on-one conversation. As much as she hated to admit it, she was desperate for a bit of alone time with him. All through the meal, all she'd been able to think about was the heat resonating off of his body and the smell of his mouth-watering cologne that kept wafting her way and taunting her nose every time he moved.

They boarded the steam locomotive that took them from Virginia City to Gold Hill and back again, and the tour guide started to drone on about the history of the area. Gina already knew the history, having been born and raised in Reno. She'd gone to Virginia City and its outlying areas every year she was in school from sixth grade onward. Heck, she could probably give the tour herself. Silver, Comstock Lode, crusty old miners, yadda, yadda…

Hayden must have known all the facts also because he turned his attention to her instead of the guide. "So," he said with a smile, "tell me about you." He slipped his arm behind her to rest it along the back of the seat, and he turned slightly so that he could look at her without craning his neck.

Gina tried to seem nonchalant even while her heart tripped over itself at the sudden nearness of him. "What do you want to know?"

"Well, I know you collect medieval weapons, and try to stab unsuspecting people with them in the dark."

She laughed. "That was so your fault."

He chuckled. "Yeah, probably." His gaze traveled over her face for a moment before a gentle smile settled on his sculpted lips. "What do you do for a living?"

"I'm a personal assistant for a bunch of very wealthy ladies."

He raised an eyebrow. "Do you like that?"

"It's all right. Not my first choice," she said with a small laugh, "but it pays my bills and allows me to travel, which is what I really love to do."

His eyes seemed to light up at her words. "Do you? Where have you been?"

"Mostly around the greater part of the western United States. I've been to a couple places back east, but not out of the country." She held up her index finger. "Yet."

"Where would you most like to visit?"

"Probably Scandinavia. Finland, Sweden, Norway...that would be my first choice."

"Why there?"

She shrugged. "I've always been fascinated with the culture. Shelby and I used to do this Viking reenactment thing, and I've kind of been into the history and such ever since."

"That would explain all the weapons."

"Partly." She gave him a playful expression. "The other reason is to, of course, try and stab unsuspecting people in the dark who are lurking on my porch."

"Well, of course."

His teasing tone and the lightness of the conversation put her at ease while setting her body on fire at the same time. He overwhelmed her with his presence and he wasn't even trying. He was laid back, easygoing, and playful, but something about Hayden seemed so roguish and wild. He reminded her of a mountain lion sunning itself. Casual and relaxed, but at any moment, all of that coiled muscle and power could spring into action. He didn't seem dangerous exactly, but there was an unmistakable rebelliousness to him that called to her in the worst way.

"So, what about you? What's your story?" she asked. "You said you were only here for the weekend. Where do you live?"

"Sacramento, currently."

"Currently. That doesn't sound permanent."

"Not much in my life is." There was a strange play of emotions across his face. A mix of rapture and sadness that tugged at her heart.

"What do you do for a living?"

The warring emotions converged back into his easy grin

and his gaze came up to rest on hers. "Is there somewhere on a business card I can put 'vagabond' or 'gypsy?'"

"I'm not quite sure that's an actual profession."

He chuckled and some of that odd sorrow came back into his eyes before he looked away. "Right now I work at a construction company, but I'm not usually in one place for too long."

She frowned in thought. "But you grew up here, right?" He nodded and she continued. "And your family lives here?"

"Just my brother. He's the only family I have." He paused before taking his arm off of the back of the seat and returning it to his side, effectively closing himself off from her. She wondered if he even realized he had done it. "Our parents died when I was seventeen," he said softly.

"Oh, I'm so sorry." Gina reached over and placed a comforting hand on his forearm. He gazed down at where she was touching him for a moment before his lips quirked slightly and he reached for her hand, taking it in between both of his and tugging her closer. Her heart picked up speed at the subtly intimate gesture. She let him twine their fingers together without a second thought. Being close to him felt so right somehow.

"Jack was only twelve when it happened," he continued. "I had always planned to go to college abroad. Didn't know what in the world I was going to study, but I wanted to do it in a far off place where I could have adventures and see amazing things. I've always had a wanderlust in me. But when our parents died..." He shook his head. "There was no one else, and I couldn't let Jack get lost in the system and be tossed from foster home to foster home until he was broken and psychologically damaged beyond repair. So, I became an emancipated minor and his legal guardian."

Gina's eyes widened and she let out a slow breath. "That's a lot of responsibility for a seventeen-year-old."

He nodded. "It was just the two of us for six years. I worked two jobs in order to pay the bills, keep us fed, and save for Jack's tuition. I became an adult with a child overnight, it seemed. Not that I ever thought of him that way. He's my little brother, you know?" He shrugged. "But still, I felt like I'd skipped over all the party years I was supposed to have, those 'best years of my life,' and woke up a dad. I didn't think much about it at the time, and I would do it all over again in a heartbeat, but once Jack started going to college and was living on campus, I didn't have anything keeping me here anymore. Jack was a grown man, pursuing his own dreams. I started to feel stifled and stagnant, and I got to a point where I felt like, if I stayed in Reno, I would be stuck here forever. One more working stiff whose dreams had died. It was overwhelming to me. I couldn't handle it. So, I took off on my bike, rode off into the sunset, and haven't been back since. Not until now. And every time I stay in a place for too long, I start to get that same stuck feeling, so I tend to move around a lot."

She sighed, digesting his words while she watched him play with her fingers and enjoyed the tenderness of his rough hands. "You know, Hayden, a place doesn't make you stuck. A place is just a place. You're only stuck if you let yourself be stuck." When he looked at her, she smiled and reached up to brush a rebellious stand of hair off of his forehead. "I admire you for what you did for your brother and the sacrifices you made to take care of him. Not everyone would have done something so selfless."

He shook his head. "There was no other choice. He's my brother. There was never any other option and never any question. Like I said, I would do it all again in a second. I don't regret any of it."

Gina's heart warmed at his devotion to his brother. "Is it strange being back here then? After being away for so long?"

"A little bit, yeah. I'm trying to figure out what that means." He chuckled, but it sounded a little forced. "What about you? Have you ever lived anywhere else?"

She shook her head. "Nope. Don't really have a desire to either."

Her statement seemed to surprise him. "But why? You said you love to travel."

"I do. I want to see every country and every culture in the world, but that doesn't mean I have to wander to do so. My family is here, and my family is everything to me. I want to go off and have an enormous adventure, but then come home and know that they are here. Family is what matters most to me. It's stability and sanity. It's home." She caught the question in his perplexed expression before he could voice it. "Reno isn't home. Reno is just a place. Just like everywhere else is just a place. If my family moved to Alaska, that would be home. This is just a place I live. The people I love are what make it home, and that's more fulfilling to me than any incredible journey." She smiled. "Sometimes, the most amazing adventures can be had right where you're standing if you have the imagination for it, and some of the greatest journeys can happen within yourself."

A bewildered sort of amazement flashed across Hayden's face as he stared at her, but she didn't look away despite the fact that her cheeks turned warm at his scrutiny. That was a philosophy she had lived by for a long time. So many people went away to "look for themselves." How could someone find who they were out in the middle of who knew where? The best place to find out who you were and what you were made of was your own environment, where you came from, where your roots were.

Hayden finally broke the silence with a short laugh. "I don't know what to do with your outlook on life. It confuses me." He gave her a boyish smile that deepened his dimple.

"Why?" she asked with a chuckle of her own.

He shook his head. "It's just so different from mine."

"Different is good." She met his gaze and arched an eyebrow in a flirty, playful gesture.

The blue of his eyes darkened and his gaze drifted to her mouth briefly before scanning over the rest of her and then coming back to her eyes. He shifted closer to her, encroaching on her space in the best way. "You're right," he murmured. "Different is very, very good."

All of her senses became full of him. He exuded raw, masculine sexuality in every ripple of movement. She wanted to run her fingers through his careless hair and trace the planes of his chest as the black fabric of his shirt stretched across it. She wanted to lose herself in his scent and his untamed presence. She wanted to bask in his confidence and soothe the momentary lines of uncertainty from his ruggedly gorgeous face.

Her gaze went to his mouth. Oh, how she wanted to sample a taste of that mouth...

"You know what I want to do?"

Shelby's boisterous voice invaded Gina's world like a siren. She and Hayden both jumped, shattering the intensity of their private moment.

Gina turned her attention to her sister, who was hanging over the back of the seat in front of them, oblivious. She sighed. "What?"

"We should go get those old western pictures done! Wouldn't that be fun?"

Gina smirked at her sister's unquenchable enthusiasm. She glanced up at Hayden, who had adopted his relaxed pose again with both arms resting across the back of the seat like he had never been rushed a day in his life.

He smiled and shrugged nonchalantly. "Could be fun, but only if you dress up like a saloon girl."

She arched an eyebrow. "What if I want to dress up like an outlaw and put a noose around your neck?"

He made a sexy purring noise in his throat. "I've never been tied up before. That could be fun too."

For all the unflappable coolness she was trying to conduct herself with, Gina couldn't help the way her face flamed at his comment. She wasn't sure if it was from embarrassment or being completely turned on.

She averted her gaze to get herself under control, then glanced up at him from under her lashes with a smirk. That roguish dimple of his was going to be her undoing.

"And fudge!"

Gina jumped again from Shelby's impeccable timing. "Excuse me?"

"Fudge!" she cried again. "We have to go to that one candy store." She turned to Troy. "They make the best fudge."

Troy nodded once.

"I love fudge. Especially divinity," Jackson threw in.

Gina shook her head at her sister's cluelessness and her heart stumbled over itself as she felt Hayden's fingers slide over hers again. She looked up at him as he picked her hand up and twined their fingers while he stared out the window as the arid Nevada desert landscape went by. He seemed lost in thought so she didn't disturb him, but when she gave his hand a little squeeze, she didn't miss the way he smiled.

Chapter Five

Hayden frowned at Troy, who was leaning up against the wall outside of the candy shop, texting. "I could have sworn that he was fun at one time," he muttered.

Gina looked up at him as she finished the piece of fudge she had purchased, and smiled. "He really is kind of a stick in the mud, isn't he? Not what you'd expect from a biker who looks like a convict."

Hayden burst out laughing and was happy they were far enough away from Troy that he couldn't hear their conversation. Gina's earlier words filtered through his mind. *"Time changes everyone."* Had time changed him? He knew it had. Time had turned him into a coward who ran from everything. His past, his family, he ran from life under the pretense of running toward it. When had he gotten so backwards? And how come he had never realized it until now? Gina had a very astute way of pointing out painful truths in the most kind and tactful manner. It didn't make those truths any less painful to come to grips with.

"You okay?"

Her gentle touch on his arm pulled him from his wandering thoughts and he turned his attention back to her. He smiled when he noticed a smudge of chocolate in the corner of her mouth. He reached out and wiped it off with his thumb, then stuck his finger into his mouth to lick it off. "Mmm," he teased. "Delicious."

Something came to life in her blue-gray eyes. Something smoldering. Something he liked. His gaze was drawn back to her wonderful lips and he lowered his head, unable to stop himself. She moved toward him simultaneously.

The door to the candy store opened and Jackson and Shelby emerged laughing. Hayden pulled away from Gina, not wanting to be razzed by his brother, and not wanting to be interrupted. When he kissed her, he wanted to indulge himself. Their attraction was magnetic and the heat that arced between them was insane. He didn't want a taste of Gina. He wanted to get drunk off of her.

He stifled a grin at her small huff of frustration and he turned to watch Jackson as he finished up an animated story that had Shelby laughing and all of her attention focused on him for the first time all day. Jack's eyes were full of life and light. He couldn't remember the last time he'd seen his brother look that way. He really liked her.

"Okay, let's go take pictures!" Shelby exclaimed once Jackson had finished talking.

Hayden reached down and took Gina's hand as they strolled down the wooden walkway, liking how she instantly responded to him. She didn't try to hold back, didn't try to hide her attraction to him. She was comfortable with it, comfortable with him. He had barely known her a day, yet she felt so familiar. As soon as he'd met her, she had been an instant fit for him. He didn't know what to do with that. It was overwhelming and frightening, but he didn't need to analyze it now. Currently, all he wanted to do was enjoy her company and her touch, and eventually, he was going to kiss her breathless.

They made their way to the Old Tyme Photo place and were ushered into separate changing areas to get garbed up for the picture. Hayden selected clothing of all black, Johnny Cash style, while Troy and Jackson went with the traditional brown and tan dusters and western shirts. All three of them donned cowboy hats and bandannas around their necks. The women were put in saloon girl outfits. Shelby's was emerald green and black while Gina's was black and maroon.

Shelby's large chest was straining against the corset almost as much as it had been straining against her leather vest. He looked over Gina while she perused the costume rack for accessories and allowed his eyes to appraise her. While she had less in the chest area than her sister, her form was still very shapely. The corset hugged her slender frame and drew attention to the curve of her hips. With an appreciative smile, and unable to stop himself, he went over to her and slid his hands around her waist. "This could prove to be an extremely distracting experience," he murmured against her ear. The smell of her shampoo tantalized him.

She stilled for a moment before she turned and draped a red feather boa around his neck. "That's the fun of it." She winked and sauntered back over to her sister. He wondered if she put more sway into her hips on purpose just to make him drool.

They gathered around the set-up in preparation for the picture. Troy sat down on a box and Hayden took a seat next to him. He caught Gina's eye as she adjusted something on Shelby, and motioned her over. "Get over here," he teased, grabbing her waist and pulling her onto his lap.

She huffed. "Regardless of my current state of dress, sir, I am a classy lady," she said with a Southern drawl.

He grinned. "That's why I picked you. I don't go for any run-of-the-mill hussy." She giggled and settled herself on his lap in a way that made him hope the photographer worked quickly before he had to explain that he didn't have a gun in his belt.

Shelby flounced her way over to Troy and flopped herself into his lap. Hayden heard him heave an exasperated-sounding sigh and he glanced over to see him looking slightly annoyed and bored out of his mind while Shelby continued to try and flirt with him. He frowned. Troy was starting to get on his nerves. He didn't remember him ever being so much of an ass. It was like, for whatever reason, he thought he was better than all of them, better than Hayden. Like he was doing everyone a favor by gracing them all with his presence. It was really annoying. And poor Shelby had been throwing herself at him all day while all he could do was grunt and nod like a friggin' Neanderthal.

"Okay, are you guys ready?" the photographer asked. "Sir, why don't you put your hand on her knee, and you put your leg up on that box in front of you." She was talking to Hayden and Gina. Gina obeyed and the photographer pulled back her skirt to reveal a lot more of her lovely toned leg. Hayden was more than willing to oblige with the photographer's request.

He glanced over at Jack, who was standing all by his lonesome over on the sidelines like the kid who got picked last for the baseball team. He kept shooting Shelby longing glances while she completely ignored the fact he even existed and tried to engage Troy, who acted like she was nothing more than annoying insect.

He snorted. "Okay, wait, I can't deal with this." He gently guided Gina off of his lap and stood. "This looks stupid. There is no motivation in this picture whatsoever. Troy and I look like we invaded a brothel and Jack is standing all alone over here like he's been benched."

Jackson scowled. "Thanks," he muttered.

Hayden waved his hands. "We need some kind of a plot or something. This just isn't working for me. Here." He grabbed Shelby by the arm and yanked her off of Troy.

"Whoa!" she cried. "Why are you manhandling me?"

He gentled his grasp. "I'm sorry. I'm just trying to fix this. You, go over here." He pushed her toward Jack and looked around at all the props. Gina's noose idea came back to him and he grabbed one, as well as an empty bottle of Jack Daniels. He looped the rope around Troy's neck and handed the end of the rope to Jackson. "You, hold that." He met his brother's eyes with a wicked smirk. Scanning the props again, he grabbed another rope and tied Troy's wrists up with it. "Okay, now, you take this and point it at him." He gave Jackson a gun and aimed it toward Troy.

"What am I supposed to be doing?" Jackson asked in bewilderment.

"Uh...you're a bounty hunter and he's an outlaw. You just captured him." He guided Shelby over to Jackson's side and positioned his arm around her waist. He tried not to laugh when he saw his brother's eyes bulge out of his head.

"Okay, so what am I?" Shelby asked.

"Uh...you're a bounty hunter too," Hayden improvised.

She frowned. "Then why am I dressed like a whore?" she exclaimed.

"You were undercover. Here, you take this." He handed her the bottle of Jack Daniels and draped the end of her black boa around Jackson's neck. "We're all bounty hunters. We caught the bad guy and now we're celebrating." He positioned Shelby's arm around Jackson's neck also and put a derringer pistol in her hand.

She made an affronted noise in her throat. "Why are you giving me the wussy pee-wee gun?"

He heaved a sigh, grabbed the derringer, and replaced it with a regular pistol. Then he grabbed a rifle for himself, went back over to his place, and eased Gina back onto his lap. He gave a curt nod to the photographer. "Okay, now we're ready."

The photographer gave him a bland expression and stared at him for several seconds. "Do you want me to cut you a check while I'm at it?" Everyone laughed and she went over to Jack to make a few minor adjustments. She made him stand on a little stool in order to make him a bit taller as he was being drowned out by feathers and Shelby's hair.

Gina looked up at Hayden while they were getting situated and gave him the warmest grin he had ever seen. "That was smooth," she whispered.

He laughed softly. "I'm sorry, I just could not continue to witness her google-eyeing Troy when he's being a douche, and watch Jack stand around like a reject. It was getting painful."

The light in her eyes was tender and she tilted her lips up to place a soft kiss on his jaw. His skin turned hot and he closed his eyes to try and get a grip. It wasn't like he'd never been around a woman before. Why did Gina's presence addle him and make him feel like a naïve kid?

"Okay, ready? Look up here. One, two, three." The photographer snapped a shot. "Okay, one more."

"Seriously, Hayden, if your hand goes any higher..."

Hayden diverted his attention down to where his hand was resting on Gina's leg. It really had moved up her thigh about three inches. He felt his face flame, something he was not accustomed to. He hadn't done that intentionally. He'd just been enjoying the feel of her skin...

"Hey, quit feeling up my sister, buddy!" Shelby snapped, half in jest...he hoped. She stepped away from Jack and put her hand on her hip, then wagged her finger at him in warning. One of the black feathers from her boa flitted through the air in front of Jack's face and he swiped at it.

"Okay, guys, get ready." The photographer went back beneath the black curtain behind the camera. "One...two..."

Jack swatted at the feather again and leaned back just enough to lose his footing on the stool he was on. He stumbled backward and toppled over, still holding onto the rope around Troy's neck, thus yanking Troy backward by the throat off the box he was sitting on. His foot made contact with Hayden's elbow on the way down.

"Ow!" Hayden exclaimed, instinctively moving away from Troy's flailing appendage. He knocked Gina off his lap and she squeaked. He reached out to grasp her and keep her from falling and his hand clamped firmly right over her breast.

"Three!"

The camera flashed.

"Oh my gosh, Jack, are you okay?" Shelby asked as she went over to him.

He shook his head as he sat up. "Yeah, but I almost broke my ankle."

"You almost broke my neck," Troy grumbled as he pushed himself back into a standing position.

"I am so sorry about that," Hayden muttered as he jerked his hand away from Gina's chest. "I was...I was trying to..."

"You were trying to cop a feel."

He groaned inwardly and couldn't bring himself to look at her as she got up off his lap. "It was reflex." He was floundering.

"Reflex to grab onto my boob?" She snorted. "Yeah, I suppose that's true for a guy."

He forced himself to stop staring at the ground, and he was surprised to find her in front of him with her hands on her hips in a sassy posture. She was smirking mischievously. Relief flooded him to see she wasn't actually angry, and he chuckled. "Wow, that was a disaster."

Hysterical laughter turned everyone's attention over to the photographer. "Oh man, this is the best picture I have ever seen!" She whooped again, and Hayden stood to go look at the proofs on her computer screen. The first picture was fine, totally normal. But the second one was chaos. Jack's cowboy hat had flown off in his descent and it was up in the air like its own entity. Troy's legs were sticking straight up as he went backward, and the look on Gina's face was pure shock at the fact that Hayden had his hand on her breast. The look on his own face was mortification. Off to the side, Shelby was staring at them all like they'd all lost their minds.

"Oh my gosh, look at my face! Look at *yours!*" Gina laughed. "That is classic! I want one of those."

"Me too," he chuckled. "I think maybe one of each for all of us."

"Holy crap!"

Shelby's sudden exclamation turned everyone's attention and Hayden blinked rapidly as his eyes fell on his brother. He had started to take off his western apparel and was only in a white wifebeater. Both of his arms were completely sleeved with colorful tattoos. "Holy crap!" he cried, echoing Shelby. "Dude, bro, when did you get all the ink?"

Jackson seemed to shrink in on himself and his face turned hot-sauce-red. "Just 'cause I'm a cop doesn't mean I'm completely straight-laced," he mumbled.

"Is *that* why you were wearing that stupid shirt?" Hayden prodded. "Why were you hiding them?" Now that he thought about it, he hadn't seen his brother's bare arms at all since he'd gotten there.

Jackson shrugged. "I didn't want you to make a big deal about it and I knew you would."

Hayden frowned. "Why would I make a big deal about it? You're a grown man, and I have tattoos of my own."

"It's not a big deal." He turned and started to head back toward the dressing rooms.

Hayden followed after him and grabbed his arm. "Wait a second, what—" He blinked in shock as his gaze fell on a familiar sight underneath his grip on Jack's upper arm. Jack had decent-sized arms, full of athletic muscle. On his shoulder he had a portrait of their mother and father on their wedding day, and below that was a portrait of Hayden himself, a younger him—a him he barely remembered. "What picture is that?" he asked, his voice coming out strangely raspy.

Jackson yanked his arm out of Hayden's grasp. "I took it at my high school graduation party," he muttered.

He perused the rest of Jackson's tattoos and raised an eyebrow as he recognized the cover art from a Metallica album adorning the other arm. "When did you start liking Metallica?"

Jackson snorted. "Gimme a break, Hayden. You used to listen to it morning, noon, and night the entire time I was in middle school."

"Yeah, I know, but you always yelled at me to turn it off. I didn't think you liked it."

"That's because you were always blaring it when I was trying to freaking study, or sleep, because some people do that every now and then." He turned and crossed his arms over his chest. He stared off to the side, a muscle in his jaw working furiously. "I have really good memories of that album, okay?"

Hayden was taken aback by his defensiveness. "Okay, that's cool. But...Jack, when did you do all of this?"

Jack snorted again, louder this time, and the tone was complete disgust. "If you were ever around, maybe you'd know, but you aren't, are you, Hayden?" He turned and stalked back over to the dressing room.

Hayden stared after him, feeling like he'd been sucker punched. He glanced back over at Gina, who shot him a concerned expression, and he followed Jack to the dressing room. He yanked the curtain aside just in time to see his brother buttoning his jeans back up.

Jackson scowled. "Thanks. Just what I want is for the entire room to see my junk." He started to pull his black shirt back on.

Hayden stopped him and took his shirt out of his hands. "Jack, wait a second."

"Why?" he growled. "Why should I do anything you say? You gave up your right to tell me what to do years ago when you rode out of here, so just save it, would you?" He snatched his shirt back.

Hayden huffed and yanked it out of his hands again. "Jack, where is this coming from? Dude, talk to me..." The pain he saw beneath the anger on his brother's face twisted his gut. "Please."

Jackson looked down, hurt mirrored in his eyes. "You just bailed on me, Hayden. You rode away and never looked back, and you haven't even cared enough to come visit me, like, ever."

"I'm here now."

"Yeah, because you ran out of excuses. I could hardly believe my eyes when you showed up in my driveway. Not when you didn't even come to my college graduation."

Hayden swallowed hard. "My work wouldn't let me off."

"Or when I graduated from the police academy."

"I did try to come to that!" he exclaimed. "My car broke down in Arizona!"

Jackson shook his head and heaved a defeated-sounding sigh. "Yeah, I know, you always had plenty of good excuses. Tons of things that were more important than me. What you never realized is that, while you thought taking care of me was sucking out all the life in your soul, I idolized you." Hayden opened his mouth to protest, but Jackson held up his hand. "Save it. Don't deny that's how you felt because I know you did. I'm not stupid. I can figure things out." He sighed again and some of the anger went out of him. "I know you did what you had to do, and I know you'd do it again, so don't give me the speech, okay? I also know it wasn't what you wanted. It was just the hand you got dealt, and you're a good person so you did what had to be done. You've always been kind and you've always been honorable, and I am forever grateful for the fact that you took the responsibility upon yourself to be my guardian. But..." He looked up at him and Hayden's heart splintered at the sorrow in his little brother's eyes. He gave a small, sad smile. "Do you know why I got that Metallica album on my arm? Because some of my most annoying memories are of when I would wake up to James Hetfield growling away instead of an alarm clock. And I'd stagger out into the kitchen to yell at you about it and there you'd be, in your badass bandanna and your black jeans with chains hanging out of the pocket, making me oatmeal and scrambled eggs. Those annoying memories also happen to me my happiest. Because you were all I had, and I knew you'd always be there. And then one day, you weren't."

Hayden exhaled a long, slow breath, wondering if he could disappear into the floorboards. He had never felt so low or small in his entire life. "Jack," he murmured. "I'm so sorry. I had no idea..." But he knew that was a lie. He'd always known. He'd just been too much of a chicken to face the guilt.

"You're the only family I have, Hayden," Jack said softly.

"Mom and Dad were taken away from us involuntarily. *You* took you away from me. They can't come back. You can, but you don't."

There was nothing in the world that anyone could have said to him that would have hurt him worse than those words. And it was because he knew they were true. Brutal, but true.

"I don't begrudge you having your own life," Jack continued. "But does that mean you have to disassociate yourself with everything from the one you used to have? Even me?"

A long silence stretched between them, mainly because the pain constricting Hayden's chest made it impossible for him to speak. Finally, Jack grabbed the shirt back again.

"You should leave it off." Hayden forced the words passed his lips. "Shelby's eyes lit up when she saw all your work."

Jack arched an eyebrow. "You think?"

Hayden nodded. "Jack," he said as his brother pushed past him to get out of the cubicle. His voice sounded as strangled as it felt. "I-I'm sorry. I—"

This time, Jack's sigh sounded like resignation. "I know, Hayden. Let's not make a federal case out of it, okay? I don't want to ruin the day, or your trip for that matter. Let's just forget it." He threw the curtain aside and stepped out.

Just forget it? How could he? He'd crushed his little brother, the person he loved the most in the whole world, because of his own selfishness, because of his own fear. He'd made him feel abandoned and not good enough. It would have hurt less if someone had bashed his knees in with a sledge hammer. Because it was all true.

He'd never hated himself more than he did at that moment.

Chapter Six

Gina frowned as she watched Jackson exit the dressing room looking troubled, followed by Hayden who looked even more troubled. While Jackson stayed and dawdled, Hayden left the store and went outside.

"What do you think that was all about?" Shelby asked.

Gina shook her head. "I don't know, but I'm going to go change so I can talk to him." She shot a glance over to Troy, who seemed oblivious, and was doing more chatting with the photographer than he had done all day.

"Did you see Jack's tattoos?" Shelby asked absently, grabbing a hold of Gina's arm. "They were glorious!"

Gina looked at her sister and smiled at the enraptured look in her eyes. "Go talk to him," she invited as she made her way back over to the dressing room. "You guys can com-pare ink." She made quick work out of changing and was happy to see Shelby looking Jackson over when she exited. She had her hands all over him as she inspected his tattoos, and he was grinning so wide she thought his face might split in half. Gina continued on outside, where Hayden was lean-ing up against a wooden support beam that held up the western awning sheltering the walkway.

She admired his broad shoulders and straight posture for a moment before she approached him and put her hand on his arm. "Are you okay?"

He heaved a sigh and averted his attention to the ground. "How much of that in there did you guys hear?"

"We were making a point of trying not to listen."

He nodded solemnly and was quiet for a long moment

before he said, "Have you ever had a moment where you hate yourself so much that you don't even want to be around you?"

Gina gave him a sympathetic smile. "We all have times like that, Hayden, but what's already happened doesn't matter. It's what you do about it that does."

He looked down at her, his beautiful blue eyes haunted and full of pain. "I hurt the person I love more than anyone," he murmured. "How do I fix that?"

"You can't fix it. All you can do is try to make it better from now on." She reached up to run her hands from his shoulders down his arms.

He captured her hands in his. "I never thought Jack would think I'd bailed on him. I don't know if I thought of anything at all aside from 'get me out of here.'" He shook his head. "I was so afraid that all my adventures would die if I stayed, that I would die, metaphorically speaking. That's what kept me from coming back, too. That fear that, somehow, I'd never find what I was looking for."

She frowned thoughtfully. "What *are* you looking for?"

"I have absolutely no idea." He gave a derisive snort. "Nice, right? I ripped my brother's heart out and made him feel abandoned so I could go off and chase some elusive, nameless thing." He rolled his eyes. "I'm starting to think maybe I'm just a selfish ass."

She squeezed his hands and smiled at him. "Anyone who did what you did for your brother can't be considered selfish."

"I don't know about that. I'm not feeling very self-sacrificing at the moment." He looked up and met her gaze. His brow furrowed. "Is it a stupid dream to always only want the wind against your face?"

His words struck Gina's heart with their truth. She understood that desire to wander, to discover and explore. It lived inside of her too. "I don't think that's stupid, Hayden. You just have to figure out what's most important to you, and then make it all work somehow." Regardless of her own wanderlust, Gina knew she could never leave her family. That had always been her number one priority. She couldn't begin to imagine her life without her parents or Shelby.

"Don't you get lonely?" she asked suddenly. "Just traveling all by yourself?"

He looked at her for a long moment, then shrugged. "I guess I never really thought about it."

"I think I'd always prefer to have a partner in crime. Someone to laugh with, get lost with, share stories with, listen to music with...eat good food with...or bad." She laughed softly as she recalled some of her more memorable trips with Shelby. "Who's going to believe your tall tales of adventure and daring-do if you don't have someone who was there to witness them with you?"

A tiny bit of sparkle returned to his eyes. "I never really looked at it like that."

She smiled and raised an eyebrow in a flirty gesture. "Maybe that's what you've been looking for. A partner in crime. You and your brother put on a pretty good show last night. You guys make a good pair."

A gentle, whimsical expression crossed his face for a moment and he nodded slowly. "I've never thought of going on a trip with Jack before. Not since we were kids. I bet he would make a good wingman." His turned his gaze back to her with a glint of devilishness in his eyes. "I can think of other people who would fit the role pretty well also." He slipped his arm around her waist and pulled her flush up against his body. The air slammed out of her lungs as his heat encompassed her and his intoxicating scent invaded her nostrils. She closed her eyes for a second to keep her head from spinning, and placed her palms against his chest.

"Where in the world did you come from?" he whispered, caressing the line of her jaw with his free hand.

"I was just minding my own business and trying to unwind after a terrible day. You were the one who invaded my house and scared me to death."

His chuckle was a deep, sexy rumble. "Jack's idiocy brought me an unexpected surprise—a beautiful woman ready to go medieval on me." She laughed and he tightened his arm around her. "I'm sorry your day wasn't good, but last night is beginning to feel like the best I've had in a very long time." His lips descended onto hers—finally—with warm, velvet contact. They played over hers in a lazy exploration that set her blood ablaze. She melted into him, lost and conquered and not minding it in the least.

The hand holding her face traveled behind her head and

tangled in her hair. He tugged a little and his tongue slid along her lower lip in a sinful caress that almost made her knees give out. She opened her mouth for him, welcomed his invasion, and found the contrasting feelings he created within her to be completely intoxicating. His arms were strong and comforting, a safe refuge, but his lips awoke an infernal, dangerous tsunami of passion within her that she knew could prove to be her undoing if she gave into it completely.

Everything about Hayden was addictive, and she was afraid of what effects that could leave on her when he picked up and went on to his next location. Was she just another experience to him? Another adventure and story to tell? When his rebel wind blew him onto the next place, would she only become a distant memory?

Reluctantly, she pulled away from his wonderful mouth and let out a soft sigh. He didn't loosen his hold on her, and tightened his fingers in her hair slightly, as if he didn't want to let her go. His gaze met hers and his eyes flashed with about as many questions as she felt.

"Gina," he rasped. "All of this is making my head spin."

The small measure of vulnerability she saw in him made her heart quiver and she reached up to run her palm across his cheek, loving the rough texture of his roguish stubble. "You don't need to hunt down all your answers right now," she murmured. "They'll come to you in time."

He didn't answer, but feathered his thumb back and forth over her jawline. His blue eyes darkened and a thousand things seemed to pass through them—troubled, confused things that she wished she could ease from his mind.

"Hey, guys, everything okay out here?" Shelby's voice tore through Hayden and Gina's personal moment—again— and Gina sighed softly as she removed herself from his arms. His hands lingered on her as he pulled away, and the fact that he so obviously wanted to remain close and connected warmed her. She couldn't deny she liked the feel of his body against hers.

"We're fine," she answered. She glanced at Jackson, who had his hands shoved in his pockets, displaying his tattoos with a proud, almost cocky posturing. Gina stifled a smile and wondered how much less awkward he felt now that he wasn't hiding and Shelby had realized he was actually a living, breathing man.

She glanced at the dynamic between Hayden and Jackson, and felt a twinge of sadness at the fact that they were looking everywhere but at each other.

"So, I saw this flyer on the door," Jackson said suddenly. "A cover band that plays classic rock and some blues is going to be performing tonight at an old bar down here. I thought maybe we could grab some dinner in a bit and then go...if you want." He shrugged, still keeping his gaze focused on the ground.

Gina glanced up at Hayden and grinned. "Do you dance, sir?" she teased.

His smile chased all the troubled shadows from his face. "When the mood strikes me." He slipped his arm around her waist and tugged her close. "Sounds like a good plan, Jack. Let's get our photos and get out of here."

They all headed back into the studio and stopped short at seeing Troy sitting on the photographer's desk, her straddling his lap, with his tongue shoved so far in her mouth Gina thought he was testing her gag reflex.

They all stared in shocked silence for a minute before Hayden shook his head and shot a glower toward Jack, who rolled his eyes and scooted protectively closer to Shelby.

"Wow," Hayden grumbled. "Unbelievable." He spotted their ready stack of pictures on the end of the desk, snatched them, and flung some cash on the desk. "That should cover it. Have a nice life, dude." He handed the photos to Shelby, who tucked them into her enormous bag, then grabbed Gina's hand and led the way back outside. "I can't believe what a jerk he's been all day," Hayden said. "I don't remember him ever being that way."

"I'm sorry," Jackson said. "It was my idea to invite him."

Hayden shook his head. "It's not your fault. None of us knew he was gonna act like a complete A-hole. He can just go home whenever he wants, or back to her place. I don't care. From this point on, he's flying solo."

"At least the picture was funny," Gina said, glancing at Shelby and trying to gauge her reaction to the current situation. She was quiet, which was never a good sign, and had her eyes downcast. Gina didn't like to see her sister look sad, especially over some lowlife guy.

Hayden reached down and squeezed her hand. He offered her an encouraging smile and a wink. "All right, let's forget all this nonsense. I know Jack only has the sports bike, but what do you say we get a little bit of riding in? Check out the scenery? When we get back, we'll grab some dinner and check out that band. Sound like a plan?"

Gina smiled at her sister. "You can ride with Hayden if you want. I don't mind the sports bike."

Shelby looked over at Jackson and shook her head. "No, it's okay. I can deal. I'll ride with Jack." She flashed him a playful smile. Gina swore she watched Jack swell to twice his normal size. "Besides, somebody's got to teach you how to ride that thing, and not like an eighty-year-old grandma." She looped her arm through his, and even though he scowled, it was obvious he wasn't seriously offended.

Gina glanced up at Hayden. He draped his arm around her shoulder and she leaned into his body as they headed back up the street. He felt comfortable next to her, and she knew she could get used to him in more ways than one. It was dangerous information to admit to herself. Especially when she knew there was no way he was going to stick around.

Chapter Seven

It was well past midnight when Hayden finally pulled into Gina's driveway. Jackson was in charge of taking Shelby home, and Hayden was reluctant to remove himself from Gina's company, not to mention her arms.

As a self-proclaimed nomad and adventure seeker, Hayden had seen a few things and had a few experiences, but something about dancing to classic rock all night in an old, rustic bar with Gina had left all previous experiences in the dust.

She was so quick to laugh, to flirt, and to tease. Her touch was a constant source of comfort and scorching desire. In all his wandering, he had never seen anyone as free-spirited as Gina, and he envied her ability to live that way without the restlessness that seemed to reside permanently in his soul.

Getting off of his bike, he removed his helmet, took Gina's, set them aside, and walked her to her door. He watched her turn the key in her lock, then took her hand and gently turned her toward him. To his delight, she rested her hands on his waist and flashed him the grin that was going to be his undoing. His heart did a somersault and his arms went around her. She leaned into him and his lips found hers before he could even think about it.

He'd meant to talk to her, to tell her how wonderful of a day he'd had despite Troy's antics and his blowout with Jackson. Instead, he monopolized her mouth, surrendering to the silken softness of her lips and losing himself in her taste. He pressed her back against the door and she held onto him tightly as she matched his passion.

"I want to see you again before I go back to Sacramento," he whispered against her lips before kissing her again.

She pulled back and looked at him with a mischievous smile. "When do you go back?"

"Monday."

She slid her palms up his chest. "Shelby will want to do something tomorrow. Street Vibrations is a weekend long party for her."

"That's great, but I want to see you alone. Just you and me. Maybe tomorrow night?"

She chewed on her bottom lip for a moment. "Do you think Jack would take my sister out for a night on the town?"

He snorted. "I think your sister could tell him to lick her boots and he'd be happy to oblige."

Gina giggled. "Have him ask her."

"Okay, what do you want to do?"

The devilment in her eyes was killing him. She gave him a flippant shrug. "Surprise me." She rose up to tease him with another kiss before she turned and escaped into her house, leaving him cold and wanting. "I'll see you tomorrow. Call me in the morning."

The smoldering yet teasing look in her eyes as she shut the door left him hot and bothered. Strange, how his body could be cold one minute then an inferno the next. This woman was going to be the end of him.

He ran his fingers through his hair several times before he finally vacated her porch.

Jackson was getting ready for bed when he finally got back to his house, and he had just enough time to propose Gina's idea to him before he grunted what Hayden assumed was an affirmative reply and vanished into his bedroom.

Despite the fact that they had all had a nice time dancing and drinking, Hayden knew his brother was still troubled. He hated that he was the cause of it.

With a sigh, he escaped onto the back porch and sat down in one of the deck chairs. He looked out at the stars shining beyond the dark silhouette of the mountains and let the silent tranquility of the night soothe him.

Gina's earlier words echoed in his mind and he contemplated them. Could he ever turn in his wandering nature and settle in one place because the people meant so much to him? He had stayed in Reno when he'd been younger because Jackson had needed him. He hadn't thought twice. And he'd never felt lonely or restless until Jack had gone to college and he'd been by himself. Sure, he'd always wanted to travel, but that ache, that stuck feeling, hadn't started troubling him until Jack had grown up. Could it be that all this time he'd been searching for peace, it had been here? Had he bailed because he missed the companionship of his brother and hadn't been able to deal with the death of his parents? Had adulthood just hit him too fast and too hard and left him so empty he'd bolted?

There were so many unanswered questions, so many truths he was afraid to look at too deeply. If he found his answers, would they rob him of his identity in the end?

He sighed and leaned back in the chair. He closed his eyes and let the crickets and the warm desert air relax him. There was one thing he *did* know—an answer he could not escape. He had been a turd to his brother. It was about time he manned up and remembered that he still had a family, and that family needed him. While he was here, he was going to make his time count.

Hayden really hoped Jackson's neighbors were understanding. It was seven o'clock in the morning—earlier than he even liked to wake up—on a Sunday, and they were going to have to be subjected to Metallica's *And Justice For All* album.

Deciding they would just have to deal, he cranked up the volume and turned it to "Harvester of Sorrow." He then ran into the kitchen to stir the scrambled eggs before they burned.

He had just put the eggs on the plate and stirred the milk into the maple and brown sugar oatmeal when Jackson came stumbling into the living room in only his boxers. His hair was everywhere and his eyes were barely open.

"What is your problem?" he grumbled, rubbing his hands over his face. "It's Sunday." He half-sat, half-flopped onto a barstool at the kitchen counter and Hayden set the plate of eggs, bowl of oatmeal, and a glass of orange juice down in front of him.

Jackson blinked a few times down at the food before understanding dawned on him and he glanced up at Hayden in surprise.

Hayden braced his arms on the counter and smiled. "Eat your breakfast, little brother. You need your strength for your big date with Shelby."

Jackson's face reddened slightly and he motioned over to the Tabasco sauce sitting on the counter by the fridge. Hayden handed it to him and he started to douse his eggs. "I don't even know what I'm supposed to do with her."

"Take her downtown. There's all sorts of stuff down there to do during Street Vibes. She'll love it."

"What are you going to do with Gina?" He stuffed a generous helping of eggs into his mouth.

"I was thinking of cooking her dinner here. Just a low-key evening. I want to get to know her better, talk to her. Everything she has to say is fascinating."

Jackson smirked and took another bite before shaking his head. "I swear on my life, Hayden. You make the best friggin' eggs ever. I can never get them fluffy like this."

Hayden grinned, somewhat surprised that Jackson's compliment made him feel warm all over. "It's the milk."

Jackson looked up at him with a frown.

Hayden pointed to the plate. "In the egg mix. I put milk in there. That's what makes them fluffy."

Jackson arched an eyebrow. "Where did you learn that?"

Hayden averted his gaze as an unexpected pain stabbed through his heart and a lump formed in his throat. "Mom."

Jackson grew quiet also and the silence stretched for several moments with only James Hetfield doing his thing in the background. "I don't remember a whole lot of her cooking," he finally admitted softly. "I don't know why. For some reason, I only remember yours."

"All of my cooking *was* Mom's." Hayden chuckled, the stabbing pain reducing to a dull, sorrowful ache.

Jackson snorted. "Yeah, okay. Mom may have taught you to cook, but she definitely did not teach you how to make that death chicken you used to force on me. I may not remember some things, but I do know that was all you."

Hayden burst out laughing. "I was trying to get the right amount of spice in the coating. I had to keep trying."

"I thought flames were gonna shoot out my mouth the first three times I ate it."

Hayden laughed harder and found the moment strangely euphoric. Better than the laughter he received from his workmates or strangers he encountered.

Jackson stabbed another bite of eggs and waved it at Hayden. "One thing I've got to give you credit for, aside from the couple times your experiments went terribly awry, your culinary creations were always to die for. I've never been able to cook like you."

Pride and warmth washed over Hayden in a wave and the satisfaction he felt at his brother's praise was a heady sensation that rivaled his greatest adrenaline rushes.

"So, what do you want to do today before *your* big date?" Jackson asked as he pushed his plate away and started on the oatmeal.

Hayden smirked and waited for his brother to look up at him before he answered. "I thought maybe we could hit the skate park."

Jackson's eyebrows shot clear to his hairline. "The one in Golden Valley we used to go to every weekend as kids?"

Hayden grinned. "Do you still have a skateboard?"

Jackson chewed, swallowed, and then looked at him like he feared for his sanity. "In the garage...you do realize neither one of us has been on a skateboard in years, right?"

Hayden shrugged. "Like riding a bicycle, right? How hard could it be? Come on, bro, live a little."

"Hayden, seriously, you need to friggin' sit down!" Jackson waved his arms in frustration and flung a pillow at Hayden as he hobbled into the kitchen to see if the water for the pasta was boiling. "You could have a concussion! You should go to the hospital!"

Adding the penne pasta to the water, Hayden turned down the heat and limped back into the living room. "I do not have a concussion, calm down," he mumbled. "I just look like the Phantom of the Opera is all." He flopped into the recliner and propped his leg on the ottoman, placing the bag of frozen peas on his grapefruit-sized knee.

Jackson put his hands on his hips and gave Hayden a measured look. "The Phantom of the Opera? Really? Not dramatic at all, are you? You just have a little scrape."

Yeah, like scraped off the whole left side of his face. It was a good thing he hadn't shaved that morning. He was pretty sure his werewolf beard was what had kept his skin on. "I'm the dramatic one? You just told me to go to the hospital."

"Dude, I can't believe you ride around on a motorcycle twenty-four-seven, but the first time you get on a skateboard after ten years, you wipe out like a noob."

"Gimme a break! I skated all day before I crashed! Give me *some* credit!"

Jackson rolled his eyes. "You should really cancel your date. Gina is gonna take one look at your road-rashed face and run out the door. And you can't even go after her because you blew out your knee!"

"Is this supposed to be making me feel better, Jack? 'Cause, newsflash, it isn't."

Jackson chuckled and shook his head. "I will never get the image out of my mind of the way your legs went up backwards over your head. It was like a reverse somersault...or a handspring off your face. I didn't think somebody's spine could bend that way."

Hayden threw the bag of peas at his brother and Jackson jaunted out of the line of fire with a hearty laugh.

To Hayden's dismay, there was a knock on the door, and he groaned.

Jackson let out another peal of laughter and went to admit Gina. "Hey, Jack," she said as she came in...wearing a knockout green dress that was short enough to make Hayden salivate. Her lustrous brown hair was hanging loose to her shoulders in lovely waves. "I thought you would have left to go get Shelby by now."

"On my way," Jack said. "I had to wait so that Gimpy over here didn't kill himself. He's on your watch now."

Hayden squeezed his eyes shut and flopped his head back against the chair.

"Gimpy?" Gina questioned.

Jackson chuckled. "Yeah, I'll let him tell you. Have fun. See you guys later."

"Yeah, you too."

Hayden heard the door close, but he couldn't look up. How embarrassing was this anyway?

"What in the world happened to you?" Gina asked in a teasing voice. He heard her move across the room toward him and stop in front of the recliner. "Oh my gosh! What did you do to your face?"

He grimaced and opened one eye just in time to see her expression of horrified concern. "I tried to pave the cement with it," he grumbled. "Thought it would look better red."

Her look of horror intensified and she flung her purse down and knelt in front of him. "Oh my goodness, Hayden! Are you okay?" Her fingers went up immediately to tangle gently in his hair, and her touch soothed the stinging in his face and the throbbing of his knee. He closed his eyes and basked in it for a moment, in her ability to make him forget everything around him but her.

"I'll live. My pride hurts more than anything else."

"What were you trying to do?"

"Ollie up to grind on a rail."

Her stroking fingers stopped and he opened his eyes to see her staring at him with mouth open and eyebrows raised. "How old are you?" she questioned.

"Old enough to know I probably shouldn't be ollying up to grind on a rail."

She laughed softly and framed his face with her palms, feather light over his scratches. Her expression softened and warmth filled her eyes. "Are you in a lot of pain?" she crooned.

Deciding to milk the situation for all he could get out of it, he stuck his bottom lip out and sniffled. "A little bit."

She giggled and brought her lips close to his. "Does this help?" She brushed a kiss across his lips, tender and teasing.

"Still hurts," he murmured.

"Hmmm..." She leaned in again and nibbled along his bottom lip, igniting his insides and causing his heart to stutter. "How's this?" She pressed her lips firmly to his.

He sighed and reached for her, pulling her onto his lap, mindful of his swollen knee. Her arms went around his neck and Hayden deepened the kiss, indulging himself. The pain vanished and the restlessness within him was nonexistent, although he actually couldn't remember it bothering him all day.

He tangled his fingers in her hair and lost himself within her sweetness, her compassion, and her astute assessment of himself and his life. Gina was an extraordinary judge of character. She saw more than anyone he'd ever met. She saw parts of him he had been afraid to examine too closely, and she made him remember what was most important in his life. She had brought a small bit of order to his chaotic existence in only a weekend. He didn't know what was better—that, or the fact that she liked kissing him as much as he enjoyed kissing her. He wanted to know more of Gina, all of Gina. A weekend was not nearly enough time.

Suddenly, the smoke alarm in the kitchen started blaring.

Hayden tensed and pulled away from Gina's addictive mouth. "Crap!" he exclaimed. "The garlic bread is burning!" He moved without thinking and knocked Gina off his lap. She rolled over the side of the recliner and landed on her butt. He launched himself out of the chair, forgetting his knee, and almost collapsed as fiery pain shot through his leg. Gina's arm around his back stabilized him.

"Whoa there, Bucky Lasek," she laughed. "Take a chill pill." She propped him up against the kitchen counter, took out the burned bread, tossed it out, and aired out the kitchen and living room. In the meantime, Hayden managed to limp to the stove, drain the pasta, and finish dinner with his remaining amount of dignity.

When the pasta had been dished up and the kitchen fanned out, Gina joined him at the dining room table. "Well, that was an adventure," she said.

Hayden glanced up at her. She was flushed and slightly disheveled from moving so swiftly and he found it incredibly sexy to see her looking so untamed. Why could he see her in every single scenario he pictured for his life? He could see her hiking next to him and camping with him in the mountains. He could see her white water rafting or horseback riding. He could see her at his side on a trip to any country he could imagine himself going to. He could even see her standing next to him, handing him a beer while he barbequed for friends and family on a weekend. It made no sense, but she just fit. Into every aspect of his life, she fit. "Gina, I have had more adventure in the last two days than I think I've had in my entire life," he replied. Her words from the day before came back to him. *"Sometimes, the most amazing adventures can be had right where you're standing if you have the imagination for it, and some of the greatest journeys can happen within yourself."*

She looked up at him and grinned, then motioned to her dinner plate. "What is this masterpiece?" she teased.

"Sausage in red wine sauce over pasta," he said, pouring them each a glass of red wine. "By the way, you must know your pro skaters."

She sat down and cocked an eyebrow at him while she sipped her wine.

"You mentioned Busky Lasek earlier. Most people with limited knowledge would say Tony Hawk since he's the most well-known. Don't tell me you used to skate too?"

"I used to play Tony Hawk Pro Skater on Playstation all the time when I was a teenager," she admitted. "That's the only reason I know anything."

He chuckled. "Yeah, well, Jack and I used to pretend to *be* Tony Hawk when we were teenagers. This morning, I woke up and decided it would be an awesome idea to try and reclaim some of that. Look what happened."

She laughed softly and reached across the table for his hand while she took a bite of the pasta. Her eyes lit up as she chewed. "Hayden, this is amazing! Where did you learn to cook like this?"

He beamed at her. "My mom initially, but I've always enjoyed experimenting in the kitchen. I used to entertain the idea of being the executive chef of my own restaurant one day."

"Used to? You don't anymore?"

He shrugged. "Yeah...I don't know why. I guess I just got too used to being a temp." He laughed, but it felt hollow, and it sounded like a lame excuse even to him. Why *hadn't* he pursued his career ambitions? What was stopping him? Fear of being stuck, or fear of failure? When had he started becoming afraid of everything? And how had he been managing to do such an awesome job of hiding it from himself? He felt like a loser. And a pansy. A pansy-loser-douchebag...who had a blown out knee and half his face left back at the skate park. This weekend was killing him.

"Hayden?"

He glanced up at Gina and only then realized she had said something. He shook his head. "I'm sorry. What?"

A strange, knowing expression crossed her face and she caressed the back of his hand with her thumb. "I said, if you want to do something, you should do it. You have nothing to lose. The only person standing in your way is yourself."

He stared at her for a moment, and the truth of her words caused his heart to clench. Ever since he'd bailed all those years ago, he'd convinced himself it was because he'd felt stuck. That his dreams had been denied because of what had happened to his parents. Well, who was denying his dreams now? He was. He was running from them. Why? Because he was lost, that was why. He'd been lost ever since Jack had gone away to college. Suddenly, Hayden's reason for existence had been gone, his routine, his life, all the things that had come to define him. He'd been left with no place and no purpose.

Crap, he had gone through some kind of weird empty nest pre-mid-life crisis because his brother hadn't needed him anymore. Except his brother *had* needed him, and he'd abandoned him. Because he was lost. Because he had no path. Because he was afraid of failing his life. Because he was freaking backwards.

He glanced up at Gina while she ate, then at where she still held his hand. He was tired of standing in his own way. He wanted those days like today with Jackson again, and he wanted nights like this with Gina. But he didn't know how to quit the life he knew. The life he knew was safe. It was cowardly, but it was his.

He had never felt so confused in his life. And he knew, pretty soon, he was going to have to pull his head out of his butt and figure it out, or else he might lose everything that mattered to him. And he'd have no one to blame but himself.

Chapter Eight

Gina couldn't remember a time when she'd ever had as much fun with a man as she'd had with Hayden over the past two days. He was kind, easy-going, and attentive. He was roguish, masculine, and rebellious, but with a gentleness that made her wish she'd met him at any other time in his life.

She wanted more than anything to see what might be possible for them if their budding relationship was allowed to flourish, but the timing was all wrong. Hayden had so much he was at war with, so much he needed to figure out. She wanted to be a partner, not a therapist, and as much as she liked him, the things he needed to deal with were things he needed to find the solutions to on his own.

She was getting ready to go home after dinner, dessert, a bottle of wine, and a leisurely evening of wonderful conver-sation, music, and erotic kissing when she got a text mes-sage from Shelby. As she looked at her phone, Hayden's went off also.

They both laughed simultaneously.

Gina glanced up at him. "What does yours say?"

He held up his phone. "From Jack. All he said was, 'oh my gosh, she is so hot.'"

She laughed. "Mine was from Shelby. Hers said, 'he's not insane as far as I can tell, which is an improvement from the guys I usually date, and he's growing on me. He has an awe-some sense of humor.'"

Hayden grinned. "Of course he's not insane. I'm the only one in this family allowed to be insane." He set down his phone and wrapped his arms around her.

Gina traced the lines of muscle on his shoulders and sighed. "You're not insane, Hayden. You just got off track is all. You'll figure it all out."

His sigh was sad, defeated-sounding. "Will you be here when I do?"

She looked up into his eyes and her heart twisted. She had been dreading this inevitable part of the conversation. "Hayden...it's dangerous for me to get my heart more involved than I already have. I like you...very much, and I can see us going somewhere...somewhere special and long-term..." She swallowed hard as sudden tears stung her eyes. "But I'm rooted here at the moment. I have my family and my job. I want to travel, but I don't want to pack up and become a gypsy...and right now, that's what you'd want me to do."

His arms around her tightened. "Whoa, wait a second. I never said I wanted you to do that, Gina. I—"

"Hayden..." She let out a slow, calming breath in order to keep herself from losing her courage. "You have so much potential. You're a wonderful man. But you're so lost." She hated the hurt reflected in his eyes. "You need to take care of those turbulent things inside of you. Your heart is split up between too many things. If you don't sort that out, your heart really isn't free to offer to anyone, is it?"

He stared at her for a long, silent moment before he shook his head and averted his gaze. "No, I guess not."

A muscle worked along his jaw and she cupped his cheek in her hand, her heart aching. "I'm not abandoning you. All I'm saying is that, until you know which direction that wind you love so much is going to blow you, I have to put the brakes on whatever this is between you and me. Otherwise, you're going to be too distracted with us to figure out what you really want, and I could get hurt. Maybe it's selfish of me, but I don't want to get hurt, Hayden."

He trapped her palm against his cheek with his hand, then brought it to his lips and kissed it. "I don't want you to get hurt either, Gina."

His voice was low and husky with emotion. The ache in her heart intensified. Why did the one man she really, *really* liked have to be in the midst of his own personal crisis? It was killing her to have to tell him any of this, as necessary as it was. She felt like she was sabotaging any potential they may have as a couple, but she also knew that she couldn't be in a relationship with a person who was only half a man. Hayden had lost himself and his path long ago. Until he found that again, she knew he would never be happy, even with her.

"Thank you, Gina," he murmured. "For the most amazing weekend of my life."

Her cheeks grew warm at his compliment and she slipped her arms around him, hugging him close. "I wish you could see yourself through my eyes," she whispered. "Or Jack's. If you could, you'd never doubt yourself again. Be careful not to go chasing after what you will never find. Pay attention to the things you already have."

He held her for a long moment, and she listened to the steady rhythm of his heartbeat. Finally, she pulled back and raised herself on her toes to press a gentle, lingering kiss to his lips. "Thank you for everything," he murmured.

"Have a safe ride home."

"I'll call you, okay?" he said.

She forced a sad smile while her mind and her heart fought a terrible tug of war. Her mind said he wouldn't, that something else would spark his interest and she would end up just another story to tell. But her heart hoped he would call, and that he would keep on calling.

"Okay." She nodded and reluctantly moved out of his embrace.

He walked her to the door, kissed her one more time, and with one last look at his beautiful face, she took off before she broke down into tears.

Hayden swore that the door closing echoed through the chambers of his heart. He stood there and stared for awhile, tingling from the aftereffects of spending the evening in Gina's presence. She filled his life in more areas than he'd realized had been empty.

With a heavy sigh, he turned away from the closed door and hobbled through Jackson's living room. He settled on the sofa and his gaze fell on a few framed pictures on the entertainment center. One of them was of their parents, the same one that was tattooed on Jackson's arm. There was one of Jackson and some of his cop friends laughing, and there was one of the two of them, taken during one of Jackson's visits—one of the many.

Jack had come to see him more times than he could count. He'd sacrificed time and money he could have spent elsewhere on him. Because he was his family. Because he was his friend. Because Hayden mattered more to him than any grand vacation or adventure. His brother had chosen to spend his adventures on him.

Some people spent their whole lives looking for that.

Gina was right. His heart was all screwed up. He had no business offering anybody anything until he stared at himself in the mirror, took a long, hard look, and asked himself if he liked what he saw.

And if he didn't, he needed to stop being a baby and start fixing problems instead of running from them.

Chapter Nine

One week later

"Shelby, I swear on my life, if you say you're cold one more time, I'm going to murder you." Gina meant it too. She looked over at her sister, who was attempting to get a fire going and failing miserably.

"Well, I am!" Shelby cried. "I seriously think we should just go charge a hotel room."

Gina closed her eyes and prayed for patience. *It's bad to strangle your sister. It's bad to strangle your sister...* "It is not my fault that you didn't come prepared. What part of 'we are camping in the redwoods' didn't clue you in to the fact that you might need to bring warmer clothes? Or maybe even a blanket with some substance?"

Shelby scowled up from where the damp wood was smoldering uselessly. "Geez, who peed in your Cheerios this morning, Crabby Patty?"

Bad to strangle your sister. "You did! By keeping me up half the night with your incessant whining!"

"I had the stomach flu, and *I was frozen!*"

Gina heaved a long-suffering sigh. Shelby bellowing at her wasn't going to get her point across any faster. "Yeah, if you'll recall, I had the flu too, and I was trying not to yak all night while you kept waking me up and wailing like an infant." She went over and yanked the matches out of Shelby's hand. "Who taught you how to build a fire anyway? Which family did you *actually* come from? Dad would be disgraced."

Shelby stepped back and put her hands on her hips.

"Now that was just rude."

Gina smirked up at her and started to reassemble the fire. She yawned. "Last night was a nightmare."

The first two days of their relaxing trip to Fort Bragg had been spent luxuriating in a bed and breakfast with a hot tub. And, of course, on the day they had to go set up their camp site in the redwoods, they'd both come down with the 24-hour stomach flu. They'd spent the entirety of yesterday trying to put up their tents—scratch that, *Gina* had spent the entirety of yesterday trying to put up their tents while Shelby had done a lot of moaning and screaming about the banana slugs that were everywhere.

To top it all off, they were in the scariest hillbilly campground they had ever seen, and in the middle of the night, some drunk dude had decided to start screaming and running around with a chainsaw. Gina had thought for a bit that Shelby was actually going to climb in the tent with her.

"Are you feeling better?" Shelby asked.

"Yeah, you?"

She nodded. "I'm actually hungry this morning."

Gina finished with the temperamental fire and sat down in a camp chair with a sigh. "Only we would end up in a *Hills Have Eyes* campground with the flu," she grumbled.

Shelby giggled and sat down also. "No kidding." Her phone beeped and she pulled it out of her pocket. She read the text message and grinned giddily.

Gina arched an eyebrow.

"It's Jack. He says he misses me, that I've been gone too long. Then he said something else I can't repeat."

Gina rolled her eyes and tried to ignore the way her heart clenched. There had been a lot of Jack this and Jack that on this trip. He and Shelby had grown rather fond of one another, and while Gina did not begrudge her sister happiness, every time Jack was mentioned, it just made Gina think of Hayden and how he had vanished like the wind he chased.

Shelby's phone beeped again and she giggled. "He says he can't stand not seeing me, that it's killing him. And that he has a surprise for me."

Gina fought the urge to groan.

"You know, *you* could call *him*," Shelby suggested. "Instead of moping around like a teenager with a crush."

The noise that came out of Gina's throat sounded like a frustrated growl. "That would totally undermine everything I said to him. He called me to tell me he'd gotten home okay. We talked then. Apparently, he had no more use for me once I wasn't around. Something sparkly must have captured his attention." She flung a twig into the fire. She knew she sounded witchy, but she couldn't help it. While she was aware of the fact that she had been the one to tell Hayden that whatever was between them needed to wait, she had been hoping she'd made enough of an impression on him to at least merit a phone call past "hey, I'm home safe," or a freaking text message. But, nothing... It was like he'd disappeared.

"If you want, I could ask Jack to—"

"No, don't say anything to Jack. I don't want Hayden to be prompted by his brother. If he doesn't want to contact me on his own, then I don't want to hear from him." Her tone was snappy to mask over the sorrow she felt at being dropped like a hot rock.

In the distance, the familiar thunder of motorcycle engines rumbled. Shelby sat up straighter in her chair. *Great*, Gina thought. *Just what I need to hear right now.* They roared closer, down the highway, through the campground, and right into what sounded like the site directly on the other side of them. Of course.

"Dude!" Shelby exclaimed. "Bikers!"

Gina twirled her finger in a circle. "Whoopee."

Shelby shot her a petulant expression and got out of her chair. "Come on, let's go look!"

Gina stared at her in bewildered shock. "Seriously? Shelby, I have had enough of bikers to last me my entire life, thank you very much."

"Oh, come on!" she cried.

"Absolutely not."

"If you loved me—"

"I don't."

"If you were my friend—"

"I'm not."

"If you were a good sister—"

"Never claimed to be."

"Gina..."

"No, Shelby! Just go by yourself. I'll start breakfast."

Shelby huffed. "Fine," she muttered, stuffed her hands in her pockets, and wandered around the trees and up the road.

Gina rolled her eyes, got up, and went to the picnic table. Like she really wanted to deal with any other biker right now. With her luck, he'd probably be hot too.

She rummaged around in the ice chest searching for the eggs and bacon. Maybe said biker next door would be a fat man with a scraggly Santa Claus beard, or a frightening man/woman who thought Shelby was a babe. That would serve her right.

She shut the lid to the ice chest and glanced up as motion caught her attention. She gasped and dropped the food she was holding. The carton of eggs bounced off the bench of the picnic table and flopped upside down. "Crap!" she exclaimed. She picked the bacon up and flung it on the table, then tried to salvage the eggs. She opened the carton and inspected. Only two had broken...but there would be a lot more if she didn't put it down. With the way her hands were shaking, she was liable to drop them again.

Strong, warm fingers covered hers, gently took the eggs, and set them on the table. "Hi," he said.

Tingles shot up her arms at his touch, and she braved a look up into his face. Bad move. He was even more gorgeous than he had been a week ago. "Hi?" she muttered. "I haven't heard squat from you in a week and all you can say is hi?" She frowned. "What are you doing here?"

He chuckled, and looking at that dimple and the sparkle in his blue eyes made her feel hot all over. That sparkle was different somehow.

"Before you kill me, please let me explain." He paused and his gaze scanned over her. He smiled softly and reached up to take her face in his hands. "Wow, I've missed looking at you. I didn't realize just how much until now."

Her heart hammered and she felt her cheeks grow hot. She had no makeup on. Zilch. And her hair was in a messy ponytail. Oh well, at least she'd brushed her teeth...and at least her lips weren't purple this time.

He shook his head. "Anyway, listen, something happened to me when I got back to Sacramento. I called you, of course, and when I got off the phone, I sat in my apartment and realized something."

She arched her eyebrows in question.

"It sucked. It was empty. I barely have any stuff because I move around so much, and it was like I was in a prison cell instead of a home. It was vacant, sterile...and then I went to work the next day and realized *that* sucked. I hate doing construction work. Why was I doing it? It made no sense to me. So, I quit."

Her eyes bulged. "Just like that?"

"Yeah, I'm a bit impulsive sometimes." He held his arms out to indicate the camp site. "As you can tell. Anyway, so then I said to myself, 'dude, what the heck did you just do?' and promptly went out and got drunk. But that also sucked because I was alone in a random bar like some kind of depressed alcoholic." He sighed. "I went home and thought about my life. I realized everything you'd said to me was true. I'd spent seven years lost and alone with no one to blame but myself. I was the reason I was restless. I was restless because I was lonely, because my life lacked meaning.

"I kept thinking about Jack, and how all the times I've felt truly content and happy over the past several years were when I was with him. And I couldn't get you out of my mind, the things you'd said and the way you made me feel. You were right. I have been looking for my partners in crime. One of those is my brother, but the other one, the one I truly want by my side to laugh and explore with, is you. You're it, Gina. I don't want to look anymore."

She stared at him, stunned. Her chest tightened to the point of pain and she bit her bottom lip as tears threatened.

He smiled and took her hands in his, pulling her closer. "I know you're upset because I didn't call you, but I had a lot going on. Plus, I knew you and Shelby were going on this trip and I thought it would be a great time for us to surprise you."

"Us?"

He nodded. "Jack is here too. He had to get gas and I didn't want to wait, so he's right behind me. Shelby's waiting at the camp site."

She couldn't help but grin as any anger she'd had toward him disappeared. "How long are you here for?"

"For as long as you are."

"No, but when do you go back to Sacramento?"

He shrugged. "I'm not."

She frowned, and her heart did something funny at the way he smiled.

"I left. Moved in with Jack. I'm going back to school. He's gonna take care of me this time."

Her confused, stilted heartbeat started to pick up speed. "You are?"

"Yup. Decided to go after that executive chef idea."

"Hayden, that's wonderful!" She threw her arms around him and held on, loving the warmth of his body, the strength in his arms, and the way he held her like she was a precious gift.

"The best part is, now I'll have someone to cook for," he murmured against her hair.

She squeezed him hard as elation rushed through her. "I want to sample everything."

He made a sexy, purring noise and pulled back slightly. "I want to sample you." He claimed her lips with his and Gina melted. There was something about Hayden. Something so different and so divine. "So, what do you say?" he whispered against her mouth. "Do you want that job as my partner in crime?"

She grinned and wrapped her arms around his neck. "Is your heart still divided?"

He shook his head and rested his forehead against hers. "My identity was always defined by my family. I just forgot that for awhile. And every part of my heart is in agreement. Every part wants to belong to you."

Now if that wasn't a good answer, she didn't know what was. She tangled her fingers in his hair and kissed him again, long, slow, sensual. Her entire body felt electric with the anticipation of many days, nights, and adventures with Hayden.

The rumble of a motorcycle caught both of their attention and she pulled back to look at him.

"Jack's here," he said with his dimpled grin.

She smiled and took his hand. "I want to go say hi."

They broke into the clearing of the next camp site right as a black Harley very similar to Hayden's pulled up. Shelby's eyes lit up like fireworks. Jack, dressed in leather from head to toe, killed the engine and removed his helmet. He got off, glanced at Gina and Hayden with a grin, then swaggered over to Shelby, oozing the confidence and sex appeal Hayden wore like a second skin. "Hey," he greeted.

She stared at him, then back at his bike. "What happened to the crotch rocket?"

"Traded it in." He hooked his thumbs into his belt loops. "Wanna go for a ride?"

Shelby chewed on her bottom lip like a schoolgirl. "Yeah, Jack. Let's go!"

His grin was wolfish. "Call me Jax."

Gina giggled, thought Shelby might jump him right there, and smiled up at Hayden. He winked at her and put his arm around her shoulder. She snuggled close and sighed. She didn't know if the world was ready for the four of them, but that was okay.

She knew it was going to be one hell of a ride.

About the Author

Brieanna Robertson

If someone were to ask me what I am, it could be summed up in one, simple word: Dreamer. Ever since I was a small child my imagination has run wild. I have been telling stories for as long as I can remember, creating grand worlds in my head and going on adventures that were invisible to others around me. Am I eccentric? Yes. Am I proud of that? Absolutely.

I write about the things that inspire me, both in this world and in realms only seen with the imagination. My heroines are sassy and strong. My heroes are sometimes shy. I have an obsession with music (and musicians) and a fascination with wings. I believe true love does exist, and sometimes it is found in the strangest, most unexpected places. I also believe that family and close friends are the glue that hold people together.

Above all things, I believe in being true to yourself and seizing the day. Life is an amazing gift. Make your experience as beautiful as you possibly can.

www.ingramcontent.com/pod-product-compliance
Lightning Source LLC
Chambersburg PA
CBHW020313150626
46552CB00022B/2865